MW01124471

Remember Well the Night

Emily Davidson

Copyright © 2015 Emily Davidson
All rights reserved.
ISBN-10: 1519261845
ISBN-13: 9781519261847

Dedication

To all those writers who take up the challenge of NaNoWriMo.
Win or lose, just keep writing.

Acknowledgments

THANK YOU SO much, Mary Fahrer, my cover looks incredible! Huge thanks is also due to the people who supported me and acted as soundboards to bounce ideas off of.

Chapter I

FOR THE MOST part, Detective Mark Jordan of Greenwich, Connecticut enjoyed his job. What he didn't enjoy was being constantly bound to his cell phone. His daughter—who was bound to her own cell phone, just not out of necessity—rolled her eyes at him.

"And, once again, work interrupts family."

"Don't speak to your father that way, Kaitlin," said Jordan's wife Lisa. "You know how hard he works."

"That's the point," Kaitlin said, frustrated by her mother's inability to grasp this. "He always talks about wanting to spend more time together as a family, but then he ends up having to leave in the middle of it."

And she got up from the table where they had been playing cards and went upstairs to her room.

Jordan shook his head as he picked up his still ringing phone.

"Detective Jordan," he said.

"I know it's your night off," came his partner's voice in his ear. "But the captain wants all hands on deck for this one."

"What happened?" Jordan asked, frowning at Detective Steven Braxton's tone of voice.

"You know that nut job they've been dealing with over in New York? The Knifer?"

"Yeah?" Jordan said, getting up from the table and walking toward the front hallway. He didn't want his wife to hear the phrase "serial killer."

"It looks like he's decided to expand his range a little bit."

"Text me the location. I'll be there soon."

As he hung up, his wife looked at him sadly. "On your night off?" she asked him.

"Criminals operate on their own schedules, honey. It's important."

"Which means it's dangerous," Lisa interpreted.

"It's just a crime scene. But I need to go."

"Be careful, OK?"

"Of course."

Jordan went upstairs to retrieve his badge and gun. On the way he stopped by the closed door of his daughter's room and knocked softly.

"I'm sorry I have to go, Kaitlin. But leave those cards where they are. Maybe we can finish up when I get back."

There was no response, so Jordan walked away. He sometimes thought dealing with murderers and other lowlifes was easier than dealing with teenage daughters.

⇥◎ ◎⇤

"Who would do something like this?" Jordan asked of nobody in particular. He had been a veteran of the police force for many years now, but something about this crime scene really got to him.

"We both know the answer to that," said his partner in reply.

"Not really," Jordan disagreed. "We know a nickname. The Knifer."

"At least there's not much doubt about why he chose that name for himself."

And there certainly wasn't. The victim—tragically young, just like all the others—had been stabbed to death, the knife left protruding from the center of her chest.

"I guess the real question is why," Detective Jordan said slowly. "I mean does this guy kill because he just likes killing? Or is there some deeper motivation behind it?"

"Let's add those questions to the list of things we'll be asking him when he's arrested," Braxton replied.

"I've got an idea," said a sarcastic voice as their captain walked up behind them. "How about we focus on catching him first before we worry about which questions to ask him? What do you think, Detective Braxton?"

"Point taken," Braxton said, looking appropriately abashed.

"Good. Now, this is Sarah Abernathy. Fifteen years old. She lived in New York, but ran away six months ago."

"Let me guess," Jordan said, "no cell phone was found with the body."

"Right in one," Captain Neil Huntington replied, nodding. "Just the same as with all the other victims."

"And we probably won't find any forensics?" Braxton asked in a tone that suggested he already knew the answer.

"The hopes are not high."

Detective Jordan knelt down to get a closer look at Sarah Abernathy. Up close, the dead girl's resemblance to his own daughter Kaitlin was even more striking. They looked to be about the same height and weight, and their ages were close as well. Detective Jordan felt a chill creep though him despite the warm spring night, but he did his best to hide it. He knew he would be off the case right away if the captain thought he had a personal connection that was affecting his on-the-job judgment. And whether it was because all the victims bore so close a resemblance to Kaitlin, or because of an outrage that so many young women's lives should be stolen away, Detective Jordan very much wanted to be a part of the team of detectives that eventually brought this guy down.

"Earth to Mark," his partner said.

Looking up, Jordan was surprised to find that he and his partner were alone; he must have been more wrapped up in his thoughts than he'd realized.

"The captain went to go talk to the medical examiner to try and find out a time of death. That would at least give us somewhere to start. Because if this case is anything like the others, forensics isn't going to give us anything useful at all."

"How is it even possible to kill someone so brutally and not leave a trace of forensic evidence?"

"That's a question for the ages," someone said from behind them. Tabitha Conners, one of their evidence techs, was walking toward them with a large, empty evidence bag.

"You've found something?" Braxton asked, with cautious hope in his voice.

"Well, not exactly," she admitted, chewing her lip under Braxton's stern gaze. Then she added, "Okay, fine. The only thing we've found is what he left us on purpose."

She gestured toward the knife and then started toward the body.

Over her shoulder she said, "If either of you are squeamish, you might want to look away."

"Please," Braxton scoffed, crossing his arms over his chest. "We're two of Connecticut's most hardened detectives."

"Why don't we go see how Captain Huntington's getting along?" Jordan suggested now. "We can figure out whether he wants us to stay here and look for evidence or get back to the station and start digging."

Braxton shrugged as if to say it made no difference to him one way or the other, but Jordan knew the nonchalance was nothing more than an act. Braxton wanted to be away from that body as badly as he did. As they walked away, they heard the wet, squelchy sound of the knife being removed from Sarah Abernathy's chest. Braxton's complexion paled a little and Detective Jordan felt his stomach clench up. He had gotten used to seeing dead bodies—a sad fact, but true nonetheless. It was just that *sound*. It made nails on a chalkboard sound like a pleasant classical symphony.

Detective Jordan turned his full attention to the present moment as they approached their captain, who was talking to the medical examiner.

"Given the state of the body," the examiner was saying, "I'd say she was only killed a few hours ago. Probably between six and seven o'clock."

"Was it done here?" Braxton asked, inserting himself into the conversation without being asked. As he spoke he took a notebook from his back pocket, flipped to the next clean page, and wrote down the estimated time of death.

"It's difficult to say for sure," the examiner answered, turning her attention to Braxton. "But if I had to guess I would say no. There's not enough blood on the ground surrounding the body."

"So why did he pick this location to bring her?" Jordan wondered out loud. From where they were standing, Main Street was easily visible. "It's like he wasn't even trying to hide it."

"Well it's not exactly unusual for a serial killer to enjoy getting attention."

"I think right now the attention should be on the fifteen-year-old girl who just lost her life," said their captain.

Detective Jordan had forgotten that he wasn't the only one who had a difficult time dealing with cases that involved young women. The captain's daughter had been even younger than Sarah Abernathy when she passed away. There was silence for a few moments; then Huntington sighed, looked up at his two top detectives, and said something that made both of their mouths fall open.

"We'll discuss the killer tomorrow morning. For now, go home and get some rest so we can tackle this thing with fresh eyes and clearer heads."

"Seriously?" Braxton asked in disbelief. "You're letting us go home? We could at least get started on something tonight."

"This case is going to be a tough one to crack so I'm going to need you both operating at peak mental capacity. I've also worked with both of you long enough to know that if you actually do get somewhere with this tonight, you won't want to stop. So go home, get some sleep, and come in early tomorrow ready to work. Understood?"

Braxton and Jordan nodded. But as they started to walk away, Jordan was struck by another thought.

"What about the family?" he asked. "They deserve to know what's happened to their daughter."

"That duty belongs with our friends from across the state line, since her legal residence was in New York. Now good night, detective."

Jordan took the not-so-subtle hint that he was dismissed and walked away with Detective Braxton by his side. He couldn't deny that he was glad somebody else would be telling Sarah Abernathy's family about her death. Since the day he'd graduated from the police academy, Jordan had always known when he would resign: on the day that he got used to informing parents that their children were dead. Something would have to be seriously wrong with his mind if delivering that kind of news didn't bother him.

By the time Jordan got home, Kaitlin was already asleep, and the cards were cleared from the table. He sat down on the couch next to his wife, who tucked her head into his shoulder.

"Was it somebody young?" she asked him after a minute or two.

Jordan hesitated before answering. It would not be wise to tell her the whole truth—that a serial killer who had successfully evaded the NYPD for months had now moved to Connecticut and was killing young women who bore many striking similarities to their own daughter.

So he just said, "Yeah. Too young. But we'll get whoever did it."

Chapter 2

JORDAN MADE SURE to eat a good breakfast the next morning, knowing he was in for a long day at the office. His daughter smelled the eggs he was cooking and came downstairs.

"Want some?" he asked, looking up from the skillet and smiling.

"Sure," Kaitlin said. She went to go put her backpack by the door and then leaned against the counter to watch him cooking. Then abruptly she said, "I'm sorry for the way I acted last night. And for the stuff I said. I know you work really hard."

"It's okay," Jordan said. "But thank you for apologizing." He scooped her eggs onto a plate and handed them to her before starting to devour his own.

"Hey, Dad? Could I have a ride to school this morning?" She gestured to the gloomy sky outside and the rain that was already drizzling from the sky. It was supposed to get worse later in the day.

"Can you get a ride home after your drama rehearsal?"

"Sure. Willow's mom or dad can take us."

"Then I'm okay with it. But I don't want you walking home, understood?"

Kaitlin frowned at him. "You haven't had a problem with it before."

"Well, I do have a problem with it now."

"It was something really bad last night, wasn't it?"

Jordan didn't reply at first. He put down his fork and took a deep breath. If the impact this case was already taking on him was so great that even his daughter could see it then maybe it would be best to go to his captain and ask to sit this one out. But when he looked at his daughter and saw all the physical resemblances she had to all the other victims, he knew he would keep his doubts to himself.

"Dad?" Kaitlin asked, looking at him shyly and a little cautiously.

"Yes, Kaitlin," he said with a sigh, coming back to the present. "It was bad. And it was very close to here. I'm not trying to scare you, but you need to be careful. So no walking home after it gets dark for the time being. Understood?"

"Yes, sir."

"Good. Now go finish getting ready."

After Jordan had dropped her off, he drove to the police station and walked up the stairs to the main room where his desk was. He was unsurprised to see that his partner was already there.

"It's only seven o' clock," Jordan said as a way of greeting. "You're on your third cup of coffee already?"

"We've got a long day ahead of us. You haven't even thanked me for your present."

"What present?"

"Top left drawer."

Jordan looked where his partner had indicated and saw a jelly-filled donut—his favorite kind—sitting atop a napkin.

"You can be an annoying, troublesome piece of work to have as a partner sometimes, but you do have your moments." Jordan helped himself to a bite and let the sweetness fill his mouth. He let out a sigh of contentment. "Thank you."

"You're welcome. I think you and I are both going to need a boost of energy to get through today."

Throughout this exchange Braxton had only glanced up briefly from the case file that was in front of him. Looking at it upside down, Jordan saw that the folder was almost empty.

"That's the start of the file from last night?"

"I wish," Braxton said. "This is all we have on the killer."

Jordan's heart sank as Braxton passed over the information for him to look at. It was certainly a quick read.

"No name. No picture. Just a list of the people he's victimized with all of their information. That's really all we have?"

"For the time being. Hopefully this file will get a lot thicker by the time we're done with it."

"No time to start like the present," Jordan said, passing the file back.

"What do you suggest?"

"Look at all the information for all the different crimes and try to find any similarities across the board. Maybe that will give us some clue as to who we're looking for."

"It's as good a place to start as any," Braxton said. Both of them knew that the cops in New York had undoubtedly already done that, so they were probably wasting their time. Then again, maybe their eyes would catch something that the people in the NYPD had missed. So they both went over to a whiteboard that was set up in the corner of the room for all the detectives to compile information about whatever case they were currently focusing their efforts on. Right away, Braxton took up a marker and wrote two words—THE KNIFER— at the top of the board. Then he created a column for each victim. Once this was done he looked at Detective Jordan, who consulted the file.

"Jessica, Katherine, Abigail, Brittany, Sarah," he read out. As he spoke, Braxton wrote each victim's name at the top of its own column.

"So what was the date for each killing?" Braxton asked, marker held at the ready.

Jordan consulted the file in his hand and read off the dates of death: February 15, March 1, March 25, April 18, May 22.

"Locations?"

Brooklyn, the Bronx, Queens, a subway station near La Guardia, a parking lot in Connecticut.

Braxton finished recording the information that Jordan had just read out loud to him and stood back to look at the board so far.

"Well that doesn't make much sense," he said after a few moments of scratching his head.

"So let's make it make sense," Jordan said, tossing the file aside. He looked at the board, lost in thought. There had to be something there, some kind of pattern. He just couldn't put his finger on what it might be.

"Why would he suddenly switch states?" Braxton asked after it became clear that neither of them were going to come up with any brilliant conclusions based on the information that was written down.

"Maybe he thought the cops there were getting too close to figuring it out," Jordan suggested.

Braxton scribbled it down on the bottom of the board. Then he said, "Maybe there's something about New York that attracts this guy. I mean all the victims lived there, including Sarah. Maybe he didn't mean to kill her in Connecticut at all; maybe he meant to tail her until she got across the state line and then something went wrong?"

"Like maybe she saw she was being followed or something and he had to jump the gun and kill her for fear of being caught," Jordan said. Even though this theory had some significant holes in it, he knew better than to just shoot down an idea before pursuing it, especially at the very beginning of an investigation.

There was a pause while Braxton stared at the board and Jordan stared at the file.

"Maybe the location's not the only thing they had in common," Jordan said. "Maybe he also had a thing for blonds. All the victims had blond hair, and they were all similar ages too: early to mid teens."

Braxton wrote this latest insight on the board while Jordan scribbled it on a blank piece of paper and added it to the file.

Getting thicker already, he thought. It wasn't much, but at least it was something.

"Blonds in their early to mid teens," Braxton muttered once he had finished writing. "Was there any evidence of sexual assault with any of the victims?"

Jordan checked the file. "No. I wonder if there was for our victim?"

"Medical examiner's report won't be back until tomorrow at least. We put a rush on the paperwork for this one, but there were a few rushes before ours."

"Which means nothing's rushed. So while we wait for that report, what should we do?"

"I'd say we should dig into the other victims' pasts. See if there's anything or anyone that ties all of them together."

"So it looks like you and I will be taking a little road trip to New York today, then? Re-interview all the families?"

"Actually, you don't have that authority because it's across state lines," Captain Huntington said, approaching them unheard from behind. "But the detectives from New York who were assigned to those cases are faxing over transcripts of interviews, copies of their notes, absolutely every last scrap of information they have. It isn't much, but maybe you'll be able to see something there that they've been missing."

"How soon will those records get here?" Braxton asked.

"They said as soon as possible. Which probably means about noon by the time they gather everything together."

"So in the meantime, we're stuck," Braxton said. Just the thought of having an open case—especially a high-profile one like this—and not being able to actually investigate made him antsy.

"Not quite," Captain Huntington corrected him. He lowered his voice as he continued, "There's a friend of mine named Jonathan Hall who knows how to do some very clever things with a computer; he might be able to help you find some information. I've told him to expect you at some point today."

"Thanks, captain."

"You can thank me if he ends up helping us solve this case." He turned to go back to his office but then stopped and said, "By the way, whatever investigating you do, make sure you keep a very low profile. The last thing we need is to cause a panic, so we don't want the media getting a hold of this. Are we clear on that?"

"Yes, sir," Braxton and Jordan both answered.

And he was absolutely right, Braxton reflected as the captain left. There was already some unease in the town of Greenwich because of what was happening in The Big Apple, so many miles away. If people found out that the killer had moved here...In a way small-town citizens were worse than people who lived in big cities, at least when it came to the way they reacted to a major crime taking place. Living in a community that was so close-knit somehow made them think that there was nothing outside of that community, that they lived in their own perfect little world where crime could never touch them.

Braxton had thought so too, as a matter of fact. He had lived for most of his life and half his career in New York City. The reason he'd moved to Greenwich, Connecticut was that he thought it would be a good change of pace, a way to make the transition into retirement a little easier. But he had quickly discovered that he was mistaken. Crime could strike anyone, anywhere, at any time.

In addition to causing panic, media coverage might also alert the killer that the police were on to him (or her). In Braxton's experience, this could have one of two possible effects: the killer either went into hiding or tried to run. From a police perspective, the killer going into hiding was only moderately positive. True, there were no more victims, no more families torn apart by grief. But what about the families of the people who had already been victimized? How were they supposed to find closure knowing that whoever killed their loved one could still be out there somewhere, biding his time and waiting to strike again?

The murderer trying to run might be a good thing in a larger city like New York, where there was a large police presence and the necessary resources to monitor any and all means of transportation into and out of the city. But in a small town like Greenwich, which lacked both manpower and resources, the most likely outcome of the criminal trying to run would be that he (or she) succeeded in getting away, and the police had to waste their time following up on a bunch of bogus leads obtained from people desperate for reward money or a few minutes of fame.

Technically, Braxton supposed there was a third option as well: whoever was killing people would turn themselves in and confess, knowing there was no chance of getting away with what they'd done. But that particular scenario was something that took place far more often on television or movie screens than in real life. And somehow Braxton thought this particular serial killer would not stop just because he was afraid of being caught.

"It would excite him," Braxton muttered out loud.

"What?" Jordan asked.

"Sorry," Braxton replied, clearing his throat and turning his focus back to the present moment. "I was just thinking out loud. The captain's right. Media coverage isn't going to do us any good for this particular case. If anything, it's going to encourage our killer to kill again. He seems to like all the attention."

"Maybe that's what made him come here," Jordan suggested, taking the marker away from Braxton and twirling it in his fingers while he thought about exactly what he should write on the board. "Maybe the media frenzy in New York wasn't enough for him. Maybe he wanted even more."

"So why doesn't he just start sending letters to the journalists? Like that Zodiac guy out in San Francisco or Jack the Ripper over in England?"

"Because he may be twisted and deranged, but he's not stupid," Jordan said, still working things out in his head while he spoke. "With all the computer science out there now, there's all kinds of ways that an anonymous letter wouldn't be so anonymous. And even though he likes the attention he gets from the media, he still doesn't want to get caught."

"So basically he's trying to strike a perfect balance between being famous—well, maybe infamous would be a better word—and having his identity shrouded in mystery," Braxton said, summing up Jordan's idea.

"Exactly," Jordan said. This time he wrote on the whiteboard and Braxton added it to the case file.

"I still don't understand why he would leave New York in the first place. Surely his crimes would get more attention there than here, wouldn't they?"

"Not necessarily," Jordan disagreed. He thought for a moment and then said, "OK. Let's say I'm the killer. I've already gotten control over New York City. I've made parents want to hide their children inside after dark for fear of me. I've made young blond women afraid to step through their doors. The entire city, maybe even the entire state, knows who I am. I'm a household name: the Knifer."

Jordan paused for a moment and Braxton gave a nod of encouragement.

"But even though I've been on national news, even though I've been blasted into every corner of the Internet and beamed straight into people's living rooms all across the United States—even though everyone in America with more that two brain cells in their skull has heard of me—I have not struck true fear into their hearts. They're far away, they don't think I can touch them."

"So he has to prove them otherwise," Braxton finished, as he realized the point his partner had been trying to make all along.

"Exactly. He wanted to expand his reputation, so he moved to another state."

"You would make a terrifying criminal, Mark, you know that?" Braxton said, writing down notes of the insights his partner had made to add to their slowly developing case file.

Jordan just smiled and shook off his partner's taunts, but Braxton was really only half joking. In all the years that they had been partners, Braxton had never seen Jordan get to the point where he might be angry enough to kill. He hated to even draw his gun, and had only done so a handful of times. And it was always to scare people, never to actually aim a shot, lethal or otherwise. But now Braxton wondered what was really going on behind those eyes.

"So what else do we have?" Jordan asked now, turning the conversation in a different direction.

Braxton shook off the vision in his head of his partner as a knife-wielding serial killer and turned his attention back to the task at hand.

Chapter 3

BY THE END of the morning, the whiteboard and the case file were both considerably more full than they had been when Braxton and Jordan had started on them. After a quick bite to eat, the two detectives decided to follow up on their captain's suggestion and contact Jonathan Hall. He worked in a small office just on the Connecticut side of the state line. Since the information from the NYPD had still not arrived, they decided to head out right then. They weren't sure how productive the meeting would be considering the small amount of information they had to go on, but at least they would be doing something more than just sitting on their hands.

Jonathan Hall was waiting outside the front door when Detectives Jordan and Braxton pulled up. He was a small, reedy looking man, whose light brown hair appeared to be thinning already despite the fact that he was still young. He spoke very fast as he shook hands with both of the detectives and introduced himself.

"You must be the two that Neil warned me about. I'm Jonathan, but please don't call me that. I much prefer Jon. Now which of you is Steve and which one is Mark?"

"I'm Steve, that's Mark," said Braxton, slightly taken aback at how readily Jon put himself on a first-name basis with them. "Our captain indicated you might be able to help us out with a case we're working on."

"We can't start the business part of this meeting yet," he said, wagging a finger at them. "I have to give you the tour first. Come on in."

The entire office consisted of a single room and a tiny little bathroom tucked away into the corner, so the grand tour took them all of about five seconds to complete. By far the most notable feature of the office was the sheer amount of electronic equipment that had been crammed into such a small space. With the exception of a modestly sized desk shoved against one wall and a few bookshelves, the entire room was filled with computer stations. Each of these stations was equipped with a monitor of a different size and various types of keyboards, mice, and printers. But apart from the computers, there was one other curiosity in the room that drew the detectives' attention: a line of yellow tape on the floor dividing the room exactly in half. Jonathan saw them looking at it and grinned.

"That's the dividing line between New York and Connecticut. So technically you could say that I work in two different states."

"Does that mean you have to pay taxes twice over?" Braxton said, a smile starting to creep across his face.

"It does actually," Jonathan replied, fighting back a grin of his own. "And of course the Connecticut ones are higher."

Both he and Braxton burst out into peals of laughter; it was almost as though they had known each other all their lives and this was some long-standing joke between them. Jordan chuckled a little, more at the extremity of his partner's reaction than at the joke itself. Normally his partner was all business during the day. It was only when he was off the job that he developed a sense of humor.

Jordan allowed the two of them approximately sixty seconds to carry on. Then he cleared his throat and said, "So Jon. Which state has the computer that's best for us?"

"Right," Jonathan said, clearing his throat and sobering up. "That would be this one over here."

He led them over to the biggest computer station of them all, situated almost in the dead center of the room. Jonathan leaned over the keyboard and pressed a few buttons; then he seated himself in the swivel chair and stared up at the screen expectantly.

"Sorry," Jonathan said, as the three of them waited for the computer and whatever high-tech software was on it to boot up. "Usually it's just me in here so that's why I don't have any other chairs. So what case is this you're working on anyhow? Neil wouldn't tell me."

Braxton and Jordan looked at one another quickly and then looked away again. Could they trust this man whom they had only just met, if even his friend the captain hadn't wanted to tell him the truth?

"It's an ongoing investigation so legally we can't tell you," Braxton said. "We just want some information about a few people."

As they had been speaking, the computer had finished loading. Jonathan pressed a few more buttons on his keyboard and a search box popped up which filled almost the entire screen.

"These are all the different criteria I can search by," Jonathan explained, indicating the long list of categories below the blinking cursor. He shoved his chair back to let them take a closer look and to give them time to think about which criteria they wanted to use.

"What do you think?" Braxton asked his partner out of the corner of his mouth.

"Addresses obviously. And maybe where they went to school? And that's elementary and high school."

"All right. That should give us a good start at least." He turned back to Jonathan. "All right, let's go with addresses and schools. At least to begin with."

"One other question before we start: how many people am I comparing?"

"Five," Jordan answered.

"I've never tried to compare five at once before…that might take the computer a while."

"How long is a while?" Braxton demanded.

"Three minutes or so," Jonathan answered. Braxton shook his head in disbelief. Days and days of police legwork, and this guy was complaining about it taking a few minutes? *What a difference a generation makes,* Braxton thought.

"That'll be fine then," Jordan said. "We have the addresses but not what schools they went to; will that work?"

"Sure," Jon answered, fingers hovering a few inches above the keys. "Just give me the info whenever you're ready."

They did so, and Jonathan pressed the "Enter" key with a flourish.

"This is some pretty advanced equipment," Braxton noted while they waited for their search results to appear. "It's all legal, I suppose, isn't it?"

"You think your captain would send you to an illegal hacker?" Jonathan asked with a grin. "He and I go way back. We have a relationship of mutual trust."

This struck both Braxton and Jordan as an attempt to dodge the question that was actually asked. Jonathan pretended to be forthcoming, but it was about information that was not strictly relevant. Still, there were some relevant bits in there, the main one being that there was no way Neil Huntington would send them to chat with a man that could not be trusted, or who was doing things without following all of the proper legal protocol.

"I just hope that if we have to use any of this information in a courtroom, the judge won't take up issue with the manner in which the information was obtained," Braxton pressed. There was a warning in his tone but Jonathan didn't seem too concerned.

"The court is falling behind the times," he responded, a faraway look in his eyes. "They may think what I do is illegal, but it's really not. All the information is out there and available on the Internet. I just have the necessary tools to get it, and those are tools that not a whole lot of people have access to. Maybe they should focus on the real criminals instead, like the ones who actually hurt people."

Before the detectives had time to think of an adequate response to that, there was a pinging sound from the monitor behind Jonathan's head. He swiveled back around in his chair to face the screen.

"Well, it looks like all of your people had home addresses within twenty miles of each other. But there's no similarities with schools, at least not across the board. Addresses 1 and 3 went to the same public school, but Address 5 lived in a different school district and Addresses 2 and 4 went to two different private schools."

"Do those schools have any staff members in common?"

Jonathan popped up another search window and typed in the question. This time the results came up much faster. Jonathan studied the screen and then said, "The two private schools had the same school board director, but the two public schools in question have nothing in common whatsoever."

Detective Braxton fished out his notebook and a pencil and jotted down the name of the school board director.

"And you compared all the staff members, right? That includes not just teachers but nurses, lunch ladies, everybody."

"Yes. And from previous years, as well."

"How is it even possible to get that much information that quickly?" Detective Jordan asked. He was mostly speaking to himself but Jonathan answered him anyway.

"That search program I just used compares archived documents from sources that I specify. In this particular case, it looked for similarities between yearbooks and staff records. This being the computer age, all that information extends several years back. I would be able to easily see, for example, if someone named John Smith dropped out of the yearbook from St. Mary's in 1996 and appeared in the yearbook from Public School 118 in 1997."

"Can you pull up a map of New York and plot the different addresses on it?" Detective Jordan asked.

In answer, Jonathan rolled his computer chair across the room to another station.

"That's why I have to have more than one machine in here," said Jonathan as he took up the keyboard for that monitor and began to type. "If I put all the different search programs I use onto one computer it would crash the server. Information overload. Or if it didn't crash it entirely, things would run very, very slowly. Unlike this, for instance."

And he pressed the "Enter" button on the keyboard, causing a satellite image of New York City to appear with five little red pins on it to indicate the location of the victims' home addresses. Jordan moved closer to that monitor, a look of intense concentration on his face.

"Can you plot the schools they attended also, possibly in a different color?" Jordan asked Jonathan.

"Steve, can you read out the addresses of the schools for me?" Jonathan asked. "They should be up in that box on the right hand side of the screen in front of you."

Braxton did as he was asked and Jon typed the information almost faster than Braxton could read it out. When he had finished, blue dots popped up on the map, along with the name of the school they represented.

"Look at this, Steve," Jordan said to his partner, but Braxton had already seen it. All of the schools were very close together, and contained within the borders that would have been made if one connected the dots that indicated the girls' home addresses. Braxton picked up the case file that they had brought with them and divided his attention between that, the screen with the map, and the first screen displaying information from the schools and the home addresses.

"Hmmm…never mind," he said to himself after analyzing the file and the two screens for a few minutes.

"What was that all about?" his partner inquired of him.

"I was just thinking that maybe a few of them might have crossed paths in order to get to school. Doesn't look like it pans out, though. Not if each of them took the most direct route, anyway."

"What if they didn't take the most direct route?" Jordan said as an idea struck him. "In fact, what if they didn't walk or take a bus at all?"

"The subway," Braxton said, catching on to the direction his partner was going in.

"Exactly," Jordan said. "Jon, can you pull up the subway lines for us?"

But he needn't have said anything, because Jon's fingers were already blazing. When this new information popped up on the screen however, all three of them were disappointed. Even if all of the victims had taken the subway to school, it looked like they would have gotten on different lines based on which stations were closest to their particular school and their particular place of residence.

"Well that was certainly less climactic than I had hoped it would be," Jordan said.

"Good try though," said Braxton. "I think we have some good suggestions for our friends on this side of the state line."

"Definitely," Jordan said. "Thank you for all your help, Jonathan. This has given us a lot of good ideas."

"Yes, thank you," Braxton echoed, shaking Jonathan's hand.

"Not a problem," Jonathan said. "If there's anything else you need, don't hesitate to get in touch. Neil knows how to get a hold of me."

"Will do," said Braxton. They turned toward the front door but Braxton stopped with his hand on the knob and turned back. "I'm sure I don't need to remind you that this meeting should remain strictly confidential."

"You have my word on that," Jonathan promised.

Chapter 4

"WE CAN'T MAKE any progress on this case!" Braxton exclaimed out of nowhere, throwing down his pen in frustration.

Jordan looked up from the case file. It had been three days since their visit to Jonathan Hall and they had virtually no new information to follow up on. As another disappointment, it turned out that they'd wasted their time with Jonathan because the New York cops had already figured those leads out on their own and followed up on everything to no avail. Legally speaking, Braxton and Jordan were only allowed to interview the people connected with Sarah Abernathy, the victim who had died in Connecticut. The NYPD had jurisdiction over the other four cases.

And the information that had been given to them—the notes and interview transcripts and so forth that the New York detectives had passed on—was not very helpful. The transcripts consisted mostly of the victim's loved ones saying how they couldn't believe she was gone, nobody would ever want to hurt her, and so on and so forth. All the members of each family had been cleared as suspects, especially once it became clear that a serial killer was at work. But with no other suspects to investigate, that was where the flow of information stopped.

"Okay," Jordan said, closing the file in front of him. It wasn't like he was getting any new information out of it anyway. He stared out the window for almost a full minute before continuing. "Okay. Maybe we're going about this the wrong way."

"We're doing everything in our extremely limited capacity to try and catch a serial killer," said Braxton in his characteristically blunt fashion. "Exactly what other approach do you suggest?"

"I suggest," Jordan answered, frowning at his partner's dismissive tone, "that we do everything in our significantly less limited capacity to solve one murder."

"If this was any other case, I'd agree with you. The best thing to do would be to dig through the victim's past, talk with her family, find any enemies she might have had. But this case is different."

"Why?" Jordan asked.

"You have been paying attention over the past few days, right? We know who killed her. We just don't know anything about him because he's nothing more than a shadow, and we can't learn anything more about him because we're wasting our time dealing with communication issues and bureaucracy."

"But how do we know it's the same guy?" Jordan pressed.

"Were you there at the crime scene? It was exactly the same as the scenes from this psycho's other murders."

"But think about it. Anyone with access to the media—by which I mean, pretty much everybody—could have found out how this guy operates. Let's face it, he does make for an interesting news story. That means pretty much anybody could have also found out how to recreate those crime scenes."

"So you think it's a copycat killer," Braxton said, picking up on his partner's point at last.

"It's a possibility we haven't considered," Jordan said. "The Zodiac killer had a copycat in a different city, why not the Knifer?"

"You're right," Braxton said after a moment. "We should leave the bureaucracy to the bureaucrats and just focus on Sarah."

"Good," Jordan said. He glanced at his watch and saw that it was almost eight o'clock at night. Without realizing it, he had just put in a twelve-and-a-half hour day at the office. Braxton had put in the same amount of time, so it was no wonder that both of their minds were functioning at a slower than normal capacity.

"Tell you what," Jordan said. "It's late. Why don't we get home and look at this with fresh eyes in the morning?"

"You know, Mark, ever since we started working this case you've been very eager to get home just after it gets dark. Why is that?"

"Like you don't already know the reason," Jordan replied, answering his partner's shrewd, insightful look with a glare. He already spent the majority of the day worrying about his daughter's safety, and he didn't need Braxton rubbing that in his face. During the time that she was at school, he felt a little better—at least at school there were plenty of people to keep an eye on her. But around mid-afternoon his attention began to lag slightly, and the darker it got the worse the lag was.

"You have every right to be concerned," Braxton said. "I'm just letting you know that if you ever want to talk to somebody about it—"

"Not here," Jordan replied sharply, cutting him off. "Here my focus needs to be on catching this guy. Everything else will fall into place after that."

"Your choice," said Braxton with a shrug. "Let's get out of here. I have a hot date tonight."

"Really?" Jordan said with a snort of tired disbelief.

"Yes. With my television."

Laughing, the pair of them packed up their things and walked away from their desks. They were almost to the staircase when their captain opened the door to his office.

"A word with you before you leave, please, gentlemen."

Braxton and Jordan followed him back into his office, both pretty confident that they knew what was coming. Sure enough, after everyone had taken a seat, Captain Huntington said, "I'd like to have a discussion about the Sarah Abernathy case. The Knifer's latest victim. Now I know you've both put in a lot of hours today, so I'll keep this brief: what progress have you made?"

"We've interviewed the victim's family and friends trying to establish motive, or whether she had any sort of connection with the other four victims," Braxton began.

"Unfortunately, that didn't get us very far," Jordan continued, smoothly picking up where his partner had left off. "According to her parents, Sarah was a perfect little angel and nobody would ever want to hurt her."

"It also turns out that the leads we got from Jonathan Hall had already been followed up on by the NYPD. We just didn't know that because they were taking their sweet time passing along the information they had."

"What leads were these?" the captain inquired.

"Mainly checking out which route the other victims took to school," Jordan answered. "If we could find some point where all four routes intersect, we might get some insight about his hunting ground."

"And serial killers normally start hunting near the place they grew up," the captain deduced, nodding slowly. "Smart. But I take it that theory didn't pan out?"

"No," Jordan said. "We did find a staff member in common between two of the schools, but he was cleared as well."

"Well, I knew going to Jon with such a small amount of information was a bit of a long shot. Still, I'd be interested to know your opinions of Mr. Hall."

"He certainly has quite the setup," Braxton said in reply.

"That he does," the captain said with a little reminiscent smile playing about his mouth.

"He's got a weird sense of humor too," Jordan said. It was the first thing to pop into his mind, and he was so tried that his internal filter wasn't functioning properly.

"I like his humor," Braxton chimed in. "It's very similar to mine."

"Which explains why I found it weird and not very humorous," Jordan replied.

Braxton looked like he was stuck somewhere between wanting to be angry or wanting to laugh. Luckily, Captain Huntington resolved his confusion by drawing both detectives back to the conversation at hand.

"I was interested more in your thoughts about his capabilities."

"The information that he's able to get does seem to be reliable," Braxton said, becoming serious once more.

"We did have a few doubts, though regarding the legality of the methods he used to collect that information."

Jordan was careful in his choice of words; he did not want to offend his captain by suggesting that Jonathan was some sort of scam artist.

"I assure you his methods are legal," Captain Huntington said. "I had similar doubts back when we first met. Then he explained to me that all of the information is available through the public domain. What he's done is create computer programs that are able to sift through all of that information and find whatever he says he's looking for."

"So we will be able to use the information in a courtroom, but it still can't help us solve this case," Braxton said in a tone of immense frustration. "Is there any way to get out of this bureaucratic nightmare?"

"Unfortunately, no," Captain Huntington said. "But Steve, you used to work in New York. Don't you still have contacts?"

"I do, and I spent a good deal of time today calling them. They all gave me the same answer: they want to help, they understand how important it is, but they can't tell me anything. Apparently Internal Affairs is in overdrive, given that it was supposedly a cop who leaked the story to the media."

"The media frenzy certainly has been causing a nightmare for them," Huntington said. "And for us, if all the attention caused the Knifer to get scared and decide to come over here."

"Actually we were thinking that he moved over here to increase his notoriety, show that he can outwit two police departments instead of just one. But there's also the possibility that the Knifer is still in New York; this could be a copycat killer."

"That's definitely one angle to explore," Captain Huntington said, nodding his approval. "But if that's the case, then we need to be focusing just on Sarah and not on any of the other victims."

"That's the conclusion we came to as well," Braxton said.

"Have you looked at the various media coverage to see what information this copycat may have been able to pick up? Or to see if there's anything that stayed the same between crime scenes even if the information wasn't released to the media?"

"Not yet," Jordan said. "We just came up with this idea a few minutes ago. We were going to look at things with fresh eyes in the morning."

At these words, Captain Huntington glanced at his watch.

"I've kept you longer than I intended," he said. "Sorry about that. I'll see you both in the morning."

Braxton and Jordan left.

⇥⊶⊷⇤

When Jordan got home, his wife got up from the couch to greet him.

"Long day, honey?"

"Yes. And not much progress either."

Legally speaking, he was not allowed to give his wife specifics about the case. Part of him found this frustrating because he couldn't vent to anybody and let out his anxieties. Then again, maybe it was best that he was being forced to separate his job from his home life.

"Don't give up," his wife told him, as she went into the kitchen to bring the plate she had saved for him.

"I never give up."

"I know that. But I also know that your job can be very stressful, especially when you're working on a tough case like this one. I can't believe that horrible man has come here."

She shivered a little and then stuck Jordan's plate in the microwave. It took Jordan a few seconds to absorb what she had just said.

"I never told you that," he said, so quietly that she almost didn't hear him.

"What was that?" she asked.

"I never told you that this murder might be connected to the Knifer."

"It was on the news," his wife said, plopping down on the couch next to him and handing over a plate of barbecued chicken. Jordan took the food absently, but he didn't move to take a bite.

"What channel did you see it on?" he demanded, perhaps a little more harshly than he had intended.

His wife frowned and answered, "Channel Seven."

The local news, then. Not the one that broadcasted information about New York as well. Just when Jordan had thought things couldn't get much worse, it looked like there was a media leak in Connecticut, too.

Chapter 5

LATER THAT NIGHT, after his wife had gone to bed, Jordan logged on to the computer and went to the website for the primary news station in New York City. Scanning the headlines, he saw that there had been no new stories about the Knifer that night. So it wasn't as if the staff of the local station had watched the news from New York City and decided to slap together a report of their own.

Now Jordan was faced with a serious dilemma: should he call his captain tonight and let him know about the situation? Or would it be better to wait until morning? After all, he wasn't sure there was much that Captain Huntington could do at this point; the report had already come on at six according to his wife, and it would undoubtedly air again on the eleven o'clock news.

Also, it was nearly 10:50 by now. Would the station really be likely to obey if the police called and told them to cancel their leading story ten minutes before it was supposed to air? Jordan thought not. There would probably just be a lot of time wasted in arguing back and forth, with the ultimate result of the story airing on TV anyway. Then again, surely the folks who worked in the newsroom were used to rolling with the punches? They could drag out the sports report or the weather or something and lead with the second story in their queue.

All Jordan knew for sure was that he needed to make a decision soon. And he couldn't call his partner for advice; that would take too much time, time he already didn't have. He took a deep breath and picked up his phone to call Captain Huntington and deliver the bad news. But before he could dial the first number it started vibrating in his hand.

"You must be a mind reader, Captain," he said when he answered it. "I was just about to call you."

"Thought my ears were burning," the captain replied. "I just saw an interesting commercial for the leading story on the eleven o' clock news tonight."

"Apparently it was on the six o'clock news as well; my wife saw the report. Is there anything we can do to stop it from airing tonight?"

"I've already called the station and talked to the manager over there. He gave me a colorfully worded lecture about freedom of speech and constitutional rights and how I wasn't worthy of being a police captain if I didn't understand these things. And then he refused to take it off the list of stories to run tonight."

"I figured something like that might happen," Jordan said with a sigh. "I still at least thought you should know about it though. I wonder how it got out? I checked the New York news station and they didn't air any stories about it tonight."

"I assume you're going to stay up and watch the report?"

"Of course."

"I am, too. See how much detail is provided; maybe that will tell us where the leak is coming from. We'll talk about it in the morning."

"Does Steve know about it?"

"He will whenever he checks his phone. He didn't pick up when I called, but I left him a message."

"He did say he had a hot date tonight," Jordan said with a grin.

"Oh really?" Jordan thought he could hear his captain smiling. "With who?"

"His television. So more than likely, he's passed out asleep on his couch. Which is exactly what I'm going to do after I watch the news. Good night, captain."

Jordan hung up and then snuck quietly over to the sofa. Just as he reached for the remote, he heard a stair creak.

Instinct took over and he froze. Or at least his body froze. His mind launched into cop mode, burning through all the possible courses of action and their likely outcomes. His gun was upstairs in the safe so he couldn't go and arm himself with that. Should he go to the kitchen for a knife? No, he thought that would make too much noise. Better to not let the intruder know he was here. If worst came to worst, he could use the hand-to-hand combat training he had received in the police academy.

He slipped quietly down to his hands and knees in the narrow space between the coffee table and the sofa. It wasn't the best position to be in if things came to a fight, but at least from here he could watch the staircase without being seen.

Creak.

That was odd…the footsteps seemed to be getting closer. As though they were coming down the stairs instead of going up them.

Creak.

Now he could see the outline of one bare foot in the darkness. A foot whose toes were adorned with the glow-in-the-dark nail polish that his teenage daughter so highly favored.

Jordan had to stop and collect himself for a moment. He had just mistaken his daughter for an intruder, had seriously considered grabbing a knife to defend himself against her. What if he had grabbed the knife? What if he had stabbed first and asked questions later? It was a terrifying possibility, and one Jordan did not care to consider. This case must have been getting to him more than he realized.

He got up and switched on the lamp that stood on the end table next to the sofa. Now it was Kaitlin's turn to freeze.

"You nearly gave me a heart attack," she said, walking down the rest of the way when she'd recovered from the shock of the sudden light.

"You nearly gave me one," Jordan replied. And now he realized that his heart was indeed beating faster than normal. "What are you doing up at this time of night anyway?"

"Dad, I'm a teenager. I haven't been to bed yet."

"Right," Jordan muttered, and ran a hand through his hair. "Sorry."

"Why do you look so spooked?" Kaitlin asked, frowning at him. "Normally you wouldn't have a heart attack if I came downstairs for a glass of water."

"Sorry," Jordan said again. "I guess I'm just letting work get the better of me. I was on the job for twelve and a half hours today. Maybe that's too long."

"Mom's been weird tonight, too." Kaitlin seemed to have forgotten her thirst because she sank down onto the couch and tucked her bare feet up underneath her.

"What do you mean?" Jordan seated himself beside her.

"Drama practice let out a little late today so I didn't get home until almost six thirty. It's only half an hour later than usual but she hugged me really hard when I walked through the door and almost started crying. She wouldn't tell me why either, and when I asked her, she just started yelling at me for not calling her if I knew I was going to be late. I mean, it's not the first time I haven't come home right on time."

That made sense to Jordan; his wife would have just seen the report on the Knifer coming to Connecticut and Kaitlin's absence, previously unnoticed, would suddenly have seemed much more important. And yet his wife hadn't told Kaitlin why she had been so frightened...obviously she only had Kaitlin's best interest at heart but Jordan thought their daughter had a right to know what was going on. Even if it scared her a little, fear could be a good thing. It could help to make her more aware of her surroundings, which might just save her life.

"If it helps, both of us have a perfectly legitimate reason for acting weird," he said, turning on the TV. "Watch the news with your old dad and you'll see why."

Right on cue, the news began. An anchor sitting behind a desk flashed up on the screen.

"Our top story tonight: the Knifer, the mysterious serial killer from New York, looks like he's moved his hunting ground. And later, what's the weather going to be like for the weekend ahead? Nelson Oliver will let you know."

Jordan shook his head. Only on the news would it be acceptable to talk about the weather right after mentioning a serial killer. After showing previews for some of the other stories that were on the list to be broadcast tonight, the anchor appeared again. Jordan leaned forward, focusing on the television screen and looking for the level of detail in the report, just as his captain had suggested.

"The Knifer has struck down another victim. Police have asked us not to reveal the victim's name because she is a minor, but we can tell you that the crime scene was very similar to those of the killer's other victims in New York. Mainly, the knife was left protruding from the victim's chest. We can also tell you exclusively that the victim had a residential address in New York City and attended high school with one of the other victims. It is unclear why this mysterious killer has moved from New York to Connecticut. If you have any information that might help police, please call this special hotline."

Jordan thought it would be the hotline number for the New York police, but he got a shock when he discovered it was the number at their precinct. Surely, *surely* Captain Huntington had not asked the news to report the phone number? If he had, then he should have at least told his two detectives who were taking the lead in this case.

Almost before the anchor finished her statement and began to move on to the next story, Jordan's cell phone started buzzing against the kitchen counter. Kaitlin, who was closer, got up to get it.

"Imagine that, your partner's calling," she said. She handed over the phone and went into the kitchen for the glass of water that she had originally come down for.

"Don't go to bed," Jordan said, before he answered the phone. "I want to talk to you, but I need to take this first."

"Okay," Kaitlin replied.

"Hello?" Jordan answered the phone.

"Are you watching the news right now? Just how many phones do you think are ringing down at the station with nobody to answer them? Why didn't the captain tell us about this? I thought he was against using the media, and rightly so, too."

"If you'll stop ranting for one second and let me get a word in," Jordan began and let the sentence hang. He heard Braxton take a deep steadying breath.

"Sorry. Go ahead."

"Thank you. The captain didn't know about the hotline; he didn't even know the story was going to air until after ten o'clock tonight."

"I guess that explains the missed call I got from him. I was asleep so I couldn't get to the phone in time. So did he try and do anything to stop it?"

"Yes, he called and spoke to the station manager. Said he got a lecture on the First Amendment for his pains. My thinking is that the station manager got ticked and slipped our number in as a hotline to get back at Huntington for asking him not to air the story."

"That could be," Braxton mused. "But how could they possibly have gotten that much detail? It's almost all the information we have. Come to think of it, did we even share that information with anyone else here? I don't think so."

"That certainly makes it seem more likely that it was the same person who's been messing things up for the boys over in New York."

"Yeah, but what's the common link between us and New York? There isn't one, is there?"

"I don't know. I don't think so."

"I think I see a visit to the news station in our future," Braxton said. "But that's going to have to wait until the morning. If I don't get some sleep here soon, I'm going to drop."

"Same here. See you tomorrow, Steve."

Braxton hung up and so did Jordan.

Jordan sighed and started to go upstairs. Kaitlin coughed behind him.

"Didn't you say you wanted to talk to me, Dad?" she asked, leaning on the counter and taking delicate little sips of water.

"Do you understand now why your mother and I were acting so weird tonight?" Jordan asked her.

"Yes. But Dad, you're a cop. You've taught me how to take care of myself."

Jordan almost revealed more information about the case, almost told her that one of the other victims had been the child of a police officer as well. Could that be a possible angle to explore? His tired mind dismissed it after a moment; after all, Kaitlin was not one of the Knifer's victims—and she never would be if Jordan had anything to say about it—so that meant only one victim had had a police officer for a parent. Hardly a motive for killing her when you considered that it wasn't a similarity shared by any of the other victims.

"Dad? You still with me?"

"Sorry," Jordan said, giving his head a little shake to bring himself back to the present moment. "I know you know how to defend yourself, and you've got a good head on your shoulders. But just promise me you'll be careful. And make sure that from now on you do call your mother if you know you're going to be late getting home. She'll probably still worry, but hopefully it won't be quite as much."

"OK. I'll be careful." She hesitated a moment, then drained the rest of her water and said, "You be careful too, all right?"

"I will. I promise. Now come on; I think it's time for both of us to get some rest."

Chapter 6

JORDAN AND BRAXTON arrived at pretty much the same time the next day. Before they had reached the top of the stairs, they heard the phone ringing. To be more precise, they heard all the phones that were in the main room ringing at once. They glanced at each other and knew immediately that this day was going to be a full-on nightmare.

"This hotline is going to stop us from making progress on any of our other cases," Detective Lynch complained as soon as he caught sight of Jordan and Braxton. "Was this your bright idea? Because I know the captain would never have done this."

"Try the station manager down at the local news," Braxton said, taking his seat. His desk, as well as Jordan's, was covered with little pink tip sheets; you couldn't even see the pile of papers that Braxton had left sitting on his desk the night before.

Detective Lynch was about to reply but the phone in front of him started ringing again. He scowled at it and then answered.

"Greenwich Police Department, Detective Lynch speaking. Yes ma'am... yes, this is the tip hotline for the Knifer...I see...Well, that's very decisive of you, ma'am, we'll be sure to look into that...No, there is no reward being offered at this time, sorry...You have a nice day. Goodbye."

"I won't bother to add to the pile on your desks," Lynch said as he hung up the phone. "Stupid lady."

"What are we sure we'll look into?" Jordan asked.

"This genius thinks that the Knifer kills his victims with a knife. She sounded so proud of herself for thinking that up, too."

"You can't be serious," Braxton said.

"Oh, but I am. And this has been going on for two hours at least."

"I guess people are watching the news before they go to work," Jordan said.

"Yep. So hopefully this is the last little rush for a while," said Lynch. Then he rapped three times on his desk.

"It'll take us all morning to sort through this mess," Braxton complained, gesturing broadly to all the little pink slips of paper.

"More like all day," said Jordan.

"We had to start putting them there after we ran out of room in the basket," Detective Lynch explained.

Braxton and Jordan turned to look towards the tip basket, which sat on the little ledge underneath the window. Normally, it only contained a few slips of paper, although it did get a little more full when they were working major cases and put out a hotline. But Jordan had never seen it like this before. There were pieces of paper spilling through the gaps in the sides and overflowing from the top; you could barely see the ledge on either side of the basket.

"Nothing to do but get started, I guess," Jordan said. He sat down, cleared a small space on the desk, and picked up a slip at random.

" 'All of Knifer's victims are women,' " he read out loud from the first one. "Write that down, Steve, it could be the thing that breaks this case wide open!"

In response, Braxton threw away a slip he had just picked up that said the exact same thing. "What I hate about tip lines," he said, continuing to sort through slips as he spoke, "is that there might actually be something worthwhile in all of this. But you have to weed out all the useless junk to find it."

Jordan knew he was right, so they both settled in for a long, tedious, time-consuming morning. But they didn't get very far before a large man with dark, oily-looking hair mounted the stairs. He looked like a hard-boiled gumshoe detective from a 1930s movie. The man stood there for a moment looking around the room. Then he asked loudly of nobody in particular, "Where are the two idiots in charge of investigating the Knifer?"

The room went very quiet and one or two officers looked rather unhelpfully in Jordan and Braxton's direction. But before anybody could say another word,

Captain Huntington's door (which stood at the head of the staircase) burst open. To his credit, the man who had shouted barely flinched.

"Good morning, I'm Captain Neil Huntington. If you'd like to step into my office, we'll continue this discussion more privately." He raised his voice and added, "Detectives Braxton and Jordan will join us."

The captain and the stranger proceeded into the office, and the usual dull roar resumed in the squad room.

"I guess that's our cue," Braxton said.

"Guess so," Jordan agreed.

"Good luck," Detective Lynch muttered as Braxton and Jordan got up and headed toward Captain Huntington's office. The tension in the room was palpable the moment the door was opened.

"Close that door if you would, please, Mark," Huntington said. Detective Jordan did as he was bidden. "This is Charles Longhorn. He's the lead investigator from New York. Charles, this is Steve Braxton and Mark Jordan. They're my best detectives and I've put them in charge of Sarah Abernathy's case."

"That the Knifer's latest victim?" Longhorn demanded, giving a curt nod to the two detectives but not offering to shake hands.

"Yes. Along with the other victims: Jessica, Katherine, Abigail, and Brittany," Detective Jordan said. He was grateful that he had read the file through enough times to memorize the names. Shouldn't this guy have done the same?

"You haven't investigated many serial killers before have you, son?" Longhorn demanded of Detective Jordan.

"I prefer to be called Mark actually," Detective Jordan said coldly. Normally he got along very well with everyone, but something about this detective from New York rubbed him the wrong way. Maybe it was the way he didn't seem to care at all about the actual victims; maybe it was the thick accent and the way he carried himself—like he was used to getting everything he wanted in life and disliked when he even had to ask for it.

"You haven't investigated many serial killers before have you, Mark?" He placed a heavy emphasis on the last word and spoke with the air of a man who is praying for patience when dealing with a misbehaving toddler. Needless to say, this only served to make Jordan dislike him even more.

"This is my first," Jordan admitted. "And hopefully my last."

"I hope it's your last, too. You sure don't know much about it."

"Why? Because I actually care about the people who have been killed? Because I know their names?"

"You can't look at them as actual people," Longhorn explained, as though he could not believe that Jordan had not grasped this point immediately. "You just have to look at them as numbers on a list. Otherwise you start taking things too personally. And that hurts your decision-making skills."

"How does caring about other people make you a worse detective? Isn't that the reason we became detectives in the first place?"

"It's the reason I did," Braxton put in before Longhorn could say anything in response to Jordan's question. "And just before you ask, I have investigated serial killers before. Caring about the victims is what always pushed me to keep going, even when I felt like giving up."

"And you think it's caring to put their stories on the local news? How do you think that helps their families get closure?"

"You can say that to us?" Braxton fired back in disbelief. "What do you think's been happening on the news in New York?"

"Enough," Huntington said loudly, breaking up the argument before it got really heated. "There was a leak here in Connecticut just like there was in New York; neither of our departments ever intended for the story to get into the media. Now can we move on to the actual reason you're here, Detective?"

But it seemed that Longhorn was not quite ready to drop the matter.

"What about the hotline?" he demanded. "If some anonymous media rat wanted to screw things up for the police department, why would he give a hotline to your precinct number?"

"We believe the hotline was established by the vindictive station manager at the news studio," Huntington explained.

"And what makes you think that?"

"The report aired on the news twice yesterday: once at six and once at eleven," Jordan chimed in. "My wife saw the report at six, and she said there was no hotline number given out then."

"I called the news station about half an hour prior to eleven o'clock last night, telling them to take the story about the Knifer out of their queue," Captain Huntington continued. "The station manager was extremely angry with me and refused to listen to my demands. Slipping in the hotline number was probably his idea of a clever way to exact revenge on me."

"And you couldn't just go down and arrest him? That's the way we would have done it in New York to make sure our demands were met."

Huntington replied, "Well no, actually I couldn't. There's this pesky thing called freedom of the press."

"I believe they have it in New York as well?" Braxton added in a nasty tone.

Longhorn's response was a scowl and a sigh. "So he can just say whatever he wants with no consequences. Freedom of the press may be great for the people, but it sure sucks for the police."

"Actually now I can arrest him," Captain Huntington said. "And I was just about to send these two to do it when you arrived and uh...announced your presence."

Longhorn finally had enough grace to look abashed, and Braxton took advantage of his momentary silence to ask, "What charges are we serving him with?"

"Interfering with a police investigation," Huntington answered. "All these tips we're getting mean you two can't devote all of your attention to solving this case, and the same goes for all the other cases we're working right now."

"Captain, what if someone actually gives a good tip?" asked Jordan. "One that ends up helping us solve this case? That would make it harder to punish the station manager for interfering with a police investigation."

"That's a bridge we'll cross if we have to. For now, bring him in, see if you can find out who his source was. Go."

"I think I'll tag along if you don't mind, captain," said Longhorn. Braxton had his hand on the doorknob but at these words he slowly drew back and turned to see what the captain would say.

"I do mind actually," Huntington replied. "I'll let you observe the interrogation, but first you and I need to have a private discussion about the best way that this arrangement is going to work."

"Fine," Longhorn said, seating himself without being invited to do so.

"What arrangement are you referring to, Captain?" Braxton asked. "He's not going to be watching our every move is he?"

"I did say it would be a private discussion, Detective," said the captain. His tone of voice told Braxton immediately that it would be no use trying to argue any further. Without another word, Braxton and Jordan left the captain's office and headed back over to their desks.

Braxton pulled out a pair of handcuffs and a set of car keys.

"Hey," Detective Lynch said, looking up as they approached. "Who was that guy?"

"Someone from New York who's assigned to the investigation of the Knifer. It's a bit unclear right now as to what exactly his role is going to be in our investigation."

"What is clear," Jordan added, "is that he's a rather dislikeable gentleman."

"I did gather that impression," Lynch replied dryly.

"Guess we'll just have to wait and see," Braxton said. "We're off to make an arrest at the moment."

"You got a suspect?"

"Not exactly. But don't worry: I'm sure you'll know when the person we're arresting arrives."

⇥◉ ◉⇤

Braxton's prediction certainly turned out to be true. The station manager, a man by the name of Levi Washington, was almost as disagreeable as Charles Longhorn, and certainly every bit as vocal with his opinions. He had several colorful names for Jordan and Braxton that he expressed on the brief car ride from the news station to the police precinct, but his personal favorite seemed to be "press freedom abusers." This was the last thing he shouted before Braxton closed him into a mercifully soundproof interrogation room and told him they would be with him shortly.

"Just take a few deep breaths," Jordan said as his partner came back into the main room.

"How about a few sips of black nectar?" Braxton suggested, going over to the coffeepot near the window. "That always helps me cool my head."

"Whatever works best for you," Jordan said with a shrug. "I vote we let our friend Mr. Washington relax for a while before we go in there."

"In other words you're like me and you want a break from having your eardrums abused."

"Pretty much, yeah," Jordan agreed easily. Braxton chuckled and took a sip of coffee.

"If we threaten him with jail time he'll probably just get together with a few of his buddies down at the station and start a free speech protest, and then we'll have another legal can of worms on our hands."

"You're probably right, there," Jordan said. He thought for a moment and then continued, "He does seem pretty self-centered."

"Completely egotistical might be a better description of him," Braxton said.

"Semantics. But however you choose to put it, the point remains the same: Levi Washington is a man who likes everything to be all about him. So let's make the interview that way. We'll reward him with his freedom if he gives up his source."

"It's as good a plan as any. Although you know as well as I do how hard it can be to get these media types to give up their sources. Still, we might as well try it. If it doesn't work, we can always try something different."

"Agreed," said Jordan. He peered toward Captain Huntington's office and added, "Shall we go and get our friend from New York and get this show on the road?"

He rose from his seat, but Braxton made no move to follow him.

Instead he said thoughtfully, "You know, Longhorn would have an awfully hard time observing the interview if he didn't know we were conducting one."

"Come on, Steve," Jordan said, frustrated at his partner's stalling. "Longhorn's not my favorite person in the world, but maybe he's had more experience dealing with these media nuts than we have. Or maybe he's already interrogated the other station managers from New York and he'll be able to tell us if something Levi says will match up with what the other guys said about their source."

"Or maybe you have an annoying habit of seeing the best in people." Braxton took one more swallow of coffee and set the half-empty cup on his desk. Then he picked up the case file and started toward Captain Huntington's office.

"I think my optimism balances out your habit of seeing only the worst in people," said Jordan, trailing along behind his partner. "I'm too trusting, you're not trusting enough. The captain knew what he was doing when he paired the two of us up."

"Can't argue with that," Braxton agreed. They reached the door to Huntington's office, knocked and were told to enter.

"We're headed to interview the station manager right now," said Braxton, addressing only his captain and looking right over Longhorn's head as though he did not exist. "We just thought you might like to know."

"Actually, you won't be doing the interview; you'll just be observing."

If Huntington was at all unhappy with this arrangement, he was certainly more adept at hiding his emotions than Braxton was.

"Excuse me?" Braxton said in disbelief, his eyebrows so high they almost disappeared into his hairline.

"I have a lot of experience interviewing guys like that nut," Longhorn explained. "Besides, I heard some of the things he was shouting at you as you dragged him up the stairs. I would have thought you'd be glad of a break from his incessant insults."

Braxton said nothing in reply because he could not deny that this was true. But he still didn't want to admit that Longhorn was right.

"What are your thoughts on getting him to talk?" Jordan asked. He was polite, and honestly curious.

"Make it all about him," Longhorn replied promptly. "Promise him his continued freedom of the press and freedom of speech on one condition: he gives up his source."

"I've interviewed guys like him before, too," Braxton said. But his tone had lost some of its maliciousness; he seemed gratified that they agreed on interrogation strategy if not on much else. "Getting him to give up his source isn't going to be easy."

"No, it won't be," Longhorn agreed. "But there is a Plan B. If he won't give up the source, we let him keep using it but tell him to clue us in on any and all communications."

"And you think he'll just keep his word?"

"Of course not. But there's a wonderful computer guru we've worked with before that will give us access to Levi's communication logs whether he knows we're getting it or not. He's a guy by the name of Jonathan Hall."

"We've met," Braxton, Jordan and Huntington said all at the same time.

"So you know what a genius he is, then," Longhorn said.

"We should still hope for Plan A to work, though," said Braxton. "That would make things a whole lot simpler."

What he didn't add out loud was that he still had his doubts about Jonathan's methods of obtaining information.

"Shall we go try and make it work, then?" Longhorn suggested, rising from his chair.

"Right this way," Captain Huntington said, gesturing them all out of his office and leading the way down the hall toward the interview rooms.

Chapter 7

"I KNEW THE guy was a pushover from the moment he walked in the door," said Levi quietly into the payphone. He glanced around to make sure nobody was paying him any undue attention, but there weren't many people out and about at almost eleven o'clock.

"How?" asked the voice on the other end of the line.

"He was a jerk at first, threatening to lose me my job, send me to jail. But he said he'd let me free if I just promised to let him know any time I talked to you. The idiot actually took my word for it."

"You're the idiot, Levi."

"Now, now, there's no need to take that tone with me." As he spoke, Levi's own tone turned more threatening. "Have you forgotten the deal we made? I keep your dirtiest secrets, and I only reveal the ones you tell me to. But I could reveal plenty more if I chose to."

"But you will not make that choice," said the person Levi was talking to.

"I could," Levi argued, trying his best not to sound whiny and defensive. But could he really reveal his source's true identity? He questioned whether or not he would have the courage. The things this man had told him…

"You could, certainly. But then you would have to admit to the police that you knew more than what you told them. I assume you lied to the police and told them you knew nothing about who gave you your information?"

"Of course I did," Levi said. "I would never give up a source."

"And yet you threatened to do just that not a moment ago," the voice on the other end of the line pointed out. "It was an empty threat, as I suspected.

Although you might be making good on it without even realizing what you're doing."

"What do you mean?" Levi asked, looking over his shoulder at the empty street once again.

"This pushover you mentioned is clearly tracking your communications somehow, trying to use them to get to me."

"I'm not as big of an idiot as you think I am," Levi replied. "I'm calling from a payphone, and there's nobody around to overhear me."

"Payphones can be tracked, too," said Levi's source.

Levi gulped. But he was used to thinking on his feet so he recovered quickly.

"Nobody in the office knows I'm making a call. They think I've just stepped out to the convenience store on the corner to buy a pack of cigarettes and have a smoke break."

"And that convenience store has a payphone outside where you're making this call right now?"

"Well yeah, but it's not in sight of the news building or anything. It's around the corner. Nobody can see me."

"No, you can't see anyone. Get off the phone now; I've got nothing else to give you anyway. And one more bit of advice: ditch your cell phone, buy one from a convenience store with cash. The next time you come begging for information, call me from that."

"And when would be a good time to reach you?"

There was silence on the other end of the phone for so long, Levi began to think that his source wasn't going to answer him.

"Tomorrow morning. And I'll call you, because I know how to cover my tracks. Send me a blank text from your new number when you get it."

Before Levi could say a word, he heard a click in his ear and then a dial tone; his source had gone. He walked back to the news station slowly, trying to appear nonchalant while looking around the whole time to make sure he wasn't being watched.

Half a block away, Charles Longhorn sat in his car, his cell phone glued to his ear. When he heard Jonathan Hall's voicemail greeting for the third time, he swore loudly, something he almost never did. Just as he tossed his phone onto the passenger seat in anger, it began to vibrate.

"What is it?" he snapped into the receiver.

"Don't act so annoyed, Charlie Boy; you called me, remember?"

"Don't call me Charlie Boy," Longhorn said, as he did in every single conversation that he had with Jonathan. "It's either Charles or Detective Longhorn, you can take your pick."

"So why were you so frantically trying to reach me?"

"I needed you to trace a call that was in progress. But the call's over now so you can't really be of any further use to me at the moment."

"Not necessarily, Detective Longhorn. Give me a second, let me get to the right computer."

"I'm surprised you're not glued to the screen," Longhorn muttered. If Jonathan heard the snide little comment he chose to ignore it.

"All right, we're up and running. Where was the call placed?"

"That's what you're supposed to tell me," Longhorn snapped. "Do you want me to do both my job and yours?"

"Let me rephrase," said Jonathan coolly. "Where was the call placed from? In other words, where are you right now?"

"Oh," Longhorn said, somewhat sheepishly. He gave Jonathan the location and heard clicking computer keys in the background.

"Payphone, huh?" Jonathan asked after a moment; his voice came out slightly muffled, as though he were pinching the phone between his ear and his shoulder.

"Yes," Longhorn confirmed.

"Well that's not going to do either of us much good."

"Why not? I thought you told me I could contact you for help with anything I needed."

"I did say that. I also explained—several times actually as I recall—that my computer programs can only access things that are part of the public record. Otherwise it turns into this little illegal venture called hacking. Payphone records aren't part of public information."

"You've done it before for me, Jon; what's stopping you this time?"

"Last time it was while the call was actually being made. Since the call has already been completed I can tell you that it lasted for two minutes and seventeen seconds, but that's all I've got."

"Great. Thanks. How about next time you try answering your phone the first time it rings?"

Longhorn hung up before he had a chance to let his temper get out of control. Levi would be in the news building for the rest of the night, so there was nothing Longhorn could do except deliver the results of his little sting operation.

Ten minutes later, he was at the police station, sitting in a room with Braxton, Jordan and Huntington. Charles Longhorn had rightly assumed that if Levi Washington thought he had gotten off scot free, the first thing he would do would be to go call his source and assure whoever it was that they were safe, they had not been exposed. That was why Longhorn had acted like a pushover during the interrogation. After Levi had been released from the custody of the police, Longhorn tailed him, waiting for him to do something suspicious. And eventually his patience was rewarded with the phone call that he had witnessed.

"I couldn't hear what he was saying," Longhorn said now. "I was too far away and reading lips isn't in my repertoire of skills. But I assume the call was to this mysterious source of his. And that idiot Jonathan Hall wouldn't pick up his phone while the call was going on, so I couldn't trace it. All he knows is the length of time it lasted."

"Well that doesn't help us much," Braxton said, stating what he thought was obvious.

But Jordan said, "Maybe it can help us."

"How, exactly? We have no means that I can see of determining who was on the receiving end of that telephone call."

"Hear me out for a minute, I'm sort of thinking this through as I go along." He paused for a moment and then continued, "Did you notice any security cameras near the payphone?"

Longhorn thought hard before answering, "No, not any that were actually focused on the phone…"

"I sense a 'but' coming," Huntington said, his tone both shrewd and hopeful.

"There was an ATM almost directly across the street from where the pay-phone was. But I still don't understand how that's going to help us."

"You can't read lips, but one of our other detectives can," Jordan explained. "If he'll consent to do so and we could get access to the ATM video from that particular time frame, we might be able to watch Levi and figure out what he's saying. Maybe he'll be dumb enough to let something slip, like a name."

"I don't know, Mark; I wouldn't be too hopeful about him being that stupid," Captain Huntington said. "But it is a good idea. If nobody has any objections, I say we go with it."

"No objections from me," Braxton said.

"Two from me," Longhorn said.

"Go ahead then," Jordan said, bracing himself to argue away anything Longhorn brought up.

"Firstly, I think Levi's source might know we're on to him, which means now Levi knows, too."

"What makes you say that?" Jordan asked.

"Toward the end, Levi started acting a little paranoid; looking around him like he was making sure nobody was watching. Don't worry, he didn't see me; I was well hidden. But it was shortly after that that he hung up and left."

"So we need to be careful about how we do this," Captain Huntington said, nodding his understanding. "And we need to be prepared for the very real possibility that there might not be as many calls flying between Mr. Washington and this source of his in the future."

"I guess that's good news and bad news for us," Braxton said. "Good news, no more media leaks. Bad news, we have a harder time catching the source of the news leak, which takes away from time we could be spending tracking down the actual killer."

"Unless they're one and the same," said Jordan. All three men stared at him. "It's not unheard of for serial killers to write letters to the media. Steve, you brought that up on our very first day of investigating. The Zodiac, Jack the Ripper; maybe our guy is following their example."

"You could be right," Braxton mused. "And it would explain why the source seems to have a lot of inside information about the way the crimes were committed."

"Alternatively," Longhorn said, "the source of the leak could be a cop. That brings me to my second objection to this plan: I have apprehensions about involving another detective."

"Seems to me that the more minds we have working on this the better off we'll be," Braxton argued. "And if this detective has the skills that we need, I don't see a reason not to make use of them."

"And the media leak didn't come from our end," Jordan added. "The information that the media got hold of for Sarah Abernathy's case is not information that was shared with anyone else. Unless you think either me or my partner is the leak?"

"That's not what I was trying to say," said Longhorn. "All I'm saying is that in my opinion the more people involved in the case, the better the chances of somebody letting something slip and the media getting a hold of it. I think we should make this case more of a need-to-know only type of thing."

"How about we try to compromise?" Captain Huntington suggested before a major argument could ensue. "We'll send whatever relevant video we find to an outside source, one that's different from any specialist that either of our departments have used during the course of this investigation. That way if the leak is coming from one of our own houses, we'll be covered."

Everyone agreed to this after thinking it over, so that was one issue at least that was resolved.

"Anyone got anything to add before we wrap this meeting up?" Huntington asked after a glance at his watch.

"Does anyone besides me find it odd that Levi is the one contacting the source?" Braxton said after a minute. "It's usually the other way around, isn't it?"

"You're right, Steve," Jordan agreed. "It makes sense that most news sources would want to remain anonymous, particularly when they're providing information about high-profile crime. But this guy…he had to at least have given Levi a phone number to reach him at."

"And Levi was definitely the one to initiate the call? It's not like the phone rang and he answered it?" Braxton asked.

"I watched him dial the number," Longhorn replied. He thought for a moment and then said, "What about this? Maybe this source only called once, meaning to remain completely anonymous. I mean after all, if the story just aired last night then this relationship hasn't been going on for very long. But Levi Washington, greedy little rat that he is, traces the number and calls him begging for more information, something else he can put out as a headline."

"But if Levi was smart enough to figure out how to do that—which, having met him, I doubt—would he really be dumb enough to use a payphone and not realize that that could be traced too?"

"It's a possibility," Longhorn said, but now he seemed doubtful of his own idea.

"I think there's another possibility," Braxton said slowly. "What if the source is just trying to distract us, to keep us from focusing all of our attention on catching the Knifer? He or she might be somehow in cahoots with the killer or has been threatened by the killer or something."

There was a brief pause as this sunk in for everybody in the room. It was Detective Jordan who finally broke the silence.

"So are we playing right into somebody else's hands?" Jordan said. "Because even if it's meant to be a distraction, catching the source will help us catch the Knifer."

"Possibly. Not necessarily. What if the source is just…I don't know, reading lines off of a teleprompter or something?" Longhorn suggested. "Let's say the source doesn't know anything beyond what he or she is ordered to spread to the media. Then we've wasted a whole lot of time and resources that we already don't have to find out nothing beyond what we already know."

"Good thing we have two police departments working on this case, then," Captain Huntington said after a moment's thought. "Longhorn, how good are you at multitasking?"

"It's part of the job description isn't it?" Longhorn replied, drawing himself up; being able to multitask was one of the things that he truly prided himself on.

"From this point on, until further notice, your main priority will be to track down the source of the media leak. Use resources from IAB, NYPD, our police department, Jon Hall—I don't care what you use to get the information, just get it and find whoever's providing insider info to the media. Meanwhile, Braxton and Jordan will be focusing on solving the murder. Just this most recent murder, mind you; we have to narrow our focus if we have any chance of succeeding."

"What if anything new comes up on the cases back in New York?" Longhorn asked. "It's not very likely, but you never know."

"That's where the multitasking comes in. You'll be working on those as well if any new information arises. I'll have a word with your captain in the morning to confirm that he's okay with that arrangement. In the meantime, I'll leave it up to you as to whether you want to stay here in Connecticut or go back to New York tonight."

"No sense wasting gas money and driving time," Longhorn said.

"Excellent," Huntington declared. "Do you have a place to stay tonight?"

Before Longhorn could answer, Detective Braxton spoke up.

"I have a comfortable couch and I know how to make excellent scrambled eggs."

"I'm lactose intolerant, so I'll have to pass on the eggs," Longhorn replied, grinning. "But I definitely wouldn't say no to a nice couch. If you had an extra toothbrush, too I'd be much obliged."

Braxton grinned. "No luck there, but I know a place where we can stop and get one."

"Good. Thank you."

"You're welcome. And I'm sorry I was so rude to you when we first met."

"Don't worry about it. I can rub people the wrong way sometimes. Or so many people have told me on multiple occasions."

With everything settled for that night, Captain Huntington dismissed the three of them with the order to get some sleep and come back ready to tackle the case afresh tomorrow.

Chapter 8

BUT IT WAS sooner than the next morning that the three of them met again. Jordan got the call just as he lay down in bed next to his wife.

"What is it, Steve?" he asked in a whisper, not wanting to wake his wife up; then, looking over, he saw that her eyes were already open, so there was no need to keep his voice down. He continued in a more normal tone, "Did you have a brainwave that couldn't wait until the morning?"

"It's Charles actually," came Longhorn's voice from the other end of the phone. "And it's not a brainwave; we have another case. I guess it's a good thing I decided to stay in Connecticut tonight."

"Is it the same perpetrator?" Jordan climbed reluctantly out of bed and stepped out into the hallway as he spoke.

"Looks like it. I've got the address."

"Hold on a minute. Let me get some paper and a pen."

He retrieved the necessary items and wrote down the address that Longhorn gave him. He shivered and tried to hide it even though there was nobody around to see. The address was only about four blocks away from his house. He could easily walk there.

"I'll be there soon," Jordan said, and then hung up. He took a moment to compose himself and then went back into the bedroom. His wife was also composing herself, sitting on the edge of the bed and looking up at him with eyes that were full of both fear and understanding. Fear for his safety, but understanding that he had to do his job.

"Is it the serial killer?" she asked.

"I won't know until I get there," Jordan replied. He hated lying to his wife, but he didn't want to worry her even more than she already was. He thought she probably saw the truth written all over his face anyway.

"Maybe one day soon we'll get to see each other when we wake up in the morning."

Jordan gave her a long, slow kiss and then set about getting dressed.

"That was to make up for the one I'll miss tomorrow," he said, slipping into khaki pants and a sport shirt.

Before he left his wife said, "One more? To hold me over?"

Jordan grinned and obliged her.

"I've really got to go now, though," he said. "Don't tell Kaitlin about this. I don't want her to worry."

"Okay."

"And don't you worry either. I'll be home for dinner tomorrow."

"I'll hold you to that. Be safe, Mark."

And then he was out the door, headed to the latest crime scene; he hoped it would be the last one of this case.

Just as with Sarah Abernathy, this girl was a dead ringer for Kaitlin. And the fact that both of the killings from Connecticut had taken place so close to his house did nothing to set Jordan's mind at ease.

"That was fast," said Longhorn as Jordan approached.

"It's a small town. Have we found anything out yet?"

"Her name is Shannon O'Neal. Lived just on this side of the Connecticut border. Beyond that, there's nothing we can do until the medical examiner and the rest of the forensic team get here."

"Maybe the sixth time's the charm," Braxton muttered.

"What?" Jordan asked, frowning.

"It was a joke," Braxton said. "One that loses its humor when you have to explain it."

"Well since you're the one that told the joke in the first place I doubt it had much humor in it to begin with," Jordan said.

"Very funny," Braxton replied dryly. "I just meant that we haven't found any forensic evidence the first five times, so maybe the sixth time is when we'll get lucky."

"Well I am half Irish," said Longhorn. "Maybe I'm the lucky charm you need."

"Lucky charm," Jordan muttered. He was unaware that he had even spoken out loud until he saw both Braxton and Longhorn staring at him. He turned away from them, wandering vaguely and looking around without really seeing anything.

Longhorn started to go after him, but Braxton caught his arm.

"This is how he gets when he's close to figuring something out about a case," he explained. "Just give him a few minutes to get it straight in his own head; he'll clue us in once he's clued in himself."

"If you say so," Longhorn said. Just then his cell phone started to ring. He looked down at it and made a face. "Oops. I forgot to tell my wife that I wasn't coming home tonight. Excuse me a moment."

And he walked away to take the call. Left alone, Braxton walked over to where the victim lay sprawled on the ground, just like all the other victims had been. Once again the knife protruded from her chest, just over her breastbone.

This guy must go through a lot of knives, Braxton thought. *Maybe we could track down the manufacturer. Unless the guys in New York have already done that? Or maybe he buys them from different places and different makers?*

Braxton pulled out the notebook that he always carried with him and jotted down these thoughts in shorthand. He knew it might not come to any type of fruition, but a bad idea was better than no idea at all. And this particular brainwave didn't actually seem all that bad. Braxton opened his mouth as Longhorn and Jordan walked up to him, but Jordan spoke first.

"There's something about luck going on here," Jordan began. "There's all sorts of rituals when it comes to luck: don't cross a black cat, throw salt over your shoulder, don't step on any cracks, horseshoes, rabbit's feet, the list goes on. But they're all rituals of a sort. And it seems to me that there's something distinctly ritualistic about these killings."

"I've dealt with ritualistic killings before," Longhorn said.

"So have I," Braxton added. "How did we miss that?"

"The placement of the weapon is exactly the same in each crime scene," Jordan said, kneeling down to get a closer look at the weapon; he was careful not to touch it and disturb the evidence. As he knelt down, one of the streetlights behind him threw his shadow across the body.

"It's a sundial," Longhorn burst out. "The knife would cast a shadow, and depending on where the Knifer was standing when he made his move—maybe that had some special significance."

Braxton made notes of all of this as Longhorn spoke, making sure they would remember it in the morning.

"It would have to be more of a moon dial instead of a sundial," Braxton pointed out. "All the victims were killed at night."

"No, the bodies were found at night," said Jordan. "How do we know he didn't kill them during the day and just positioned them at night?"

"I can tell you when she died," said a voice from right behind them. The medical examiner had arrived. "Or at least give you a rough estimate. But first I'll need you three to kindly get out of my way."

Longhorn, Jordan and Braxton hastened to do as they were told.

"Preliminary time of death is two to three hours ago," said the medical examiner after checking her equipment.

"After the sun went down," Braxton said with a sigh.

He told one of the photographers who was passing to make sure the body was photographed from all angles. The photographer in turn snapped back that she didn't appreciate being told how to do her job. Longhorn looked closely at the young woman's pale face, at the way she was putting off taking pictures of the body for as long as possible.

"Is this your first crime scene?" he asked her kindly. The girl burst into tears and fell into his opened arms.

"It's not my first," she gasped out. "It's just that most of the time the victims don't look like my best friend's teenage daughter. I had just gotten home from having dinner with them when I got the call to come here. I mean, it isn't her, it isn't my friend's daughter but still…"

She broke off into little sniffles.

"Sorry I snapped at you, Detective Braxton," she said after a moment. "I'll make sure the body gets photographed properly."

"You go home and get some rest," Braxton told her. "There are plenty of other people with cameras here."

"Yeah, and they're all assigned to take photos of other things. We all work according to a system, you know. I'll stay. Besides, I want to do my part to help catch this creep, whoever he is."

And she turned away, her camera raised to her face, doing her job quickly but carefully.

"You're a man who's full of surprises, Charles Longhorn," said Braxton.

"I briefly worked as part of a forensics team while I was still studying to be a detective. I remember how I felt at my first gruesome murder scene. I think I had the same look on my face that she just had."

Maybe he's not so bad after all, Braxton thought to himself. *Maybe my first impression of him was wrong.*

Detective Longhorn continued to prove his worth the next morning.

"I had an idea last night," he said as he and Braxton walked up to where Jordan was already seated at the desk. "That comment I made off the cuff at the crime scene the other night—the one that sparked your brainwave about luck? I think these killings may have something to do with Irish mythology."

"Do you have any support for this theory or is it just a wild guess?" Jordan asked; but he wrote down "Irish lore" on the whiteboard next to him as he spoke.

"I don't have any support yet, but I can get some. I've got some old books about Celtic myth at my place back in New York. I have to go back up there today and get a few things, so I figured I would bring those along as well."

"But what put you onto the idea of Irish mythology in the first place?" Jordan asked.

"The way Mark's shadow crossed the body," Longhorn explained. "At Stonehenge in England, the sun casts a unique shadow on the summer solstice, June 21st. Something about the way the rocks are positioned or something, I don't really know all the specifics. And there are all sorts of theories about *why* the rocks were positioned that way. But everyone generally agrees that if you see the sunrise on that day and see the way the light falls as it bounces off the rocks, then you'll receive a very high dose of good luck for the coming year."

"I thought Stonehenge was used as a sort of almanac," Jordan said. "Helped the farmers over there know when the best time to plant and harvest their crops was."

"That's certainly the most popular theory. But another one is that this ancient group called the Druids made Stonehenge and it had some sort of mystical significance for them. One thing sort of led to another from there."

"Impressive," Jordan said. "I say we should run with it. You said you have reference books at home?"

"Yes. And I know this isn't technically my case, but I appreciate you letting me provide some input."

"Believe me, we're the ones who appreciate your input," Braxton said. Jordan nodded his agreement but something seemed strangely off to him; was his partner being almost too kind? "We would also appreciate it if you could bring any crime scene photos you have from the other murders."

"Sure. But don't you already have them? I thought I sent them over with everything else."

"You did," Braxton replied. "But those were just copies. If we're playing with light and shadow, it might help to see the originals."

"Good thinking," Longhorn said. He glanced at his watch and added, "If I leave now I should be able to get back some time early this afternoon. Just in time to drop the information off to you and start tailing our delightful friend Mr. Washington. See if he's dumb enough to make another call to his source."

He said goodbye to the two detectives and left. Jordan waited until he was gone to turn to his partner.

"You're in a strangely pleasant mood this morning."

"What do you mean by that? I'm always in a pleasant mood."

"Come on, spill the beans already. Yesterday you hated the guy's guts, now you're going out of your way to be kind and welcoming. Why is that?"

"I do think he could help us solve this case," said Braxton. "But I also think I'm not the only one who's been acting strangely lately."

"How has he been acting weird?" Jordan asked.

"Last night at the crime scene, while you were taking your little walk to sort things out in your head, he stepped away to take a phone call from his wife. He said he'd forgotten to tell her that he would be spending the night in Connecticut."

"So?" Jordan asked. "My wife would be calling me too if I didn't show up at home and she didn't know where I was."

"Funny thing is, I could have sworn I heard him talking to his wife earlier, after the two of us got to my place."

"And did he mention anything about staying in Connecticut for the night?"

"Well…come to think of it, no he didn't. But don't you think it's just a bit odd that the day he shows up, another murder happens? And being here certainly puts him in a good position to get information about how the investigation is going."

"Are you saying he's the media leak or the killer?" Jordan asked, being careful to keep the scoffing tone out of his voice.

"They could be one and the same, remember?"

"Him being the source of the leak I might be able to buy," Jordan said after some thought. "It's doubtful, but it's still in the range of possibilities. But there's no way he's the killer. He was with us the whole afternoon."

But it seemed Braxton had been well prepared for Jordan to make that counterargument.

"The medical examiner said the girl was killed at about seven or eight o'clock. That would have been right around the time that Longhorn was tailing Levi. Which, as you'll recall, he insisted on doing alone."

That was a bit suspicious, Jordan had to admit. But he was still more than a little skeptical.

"What do you want to do? Send someone to tail him?"

"He'd catch on to it right away," said Braxton, shaking his head. "And we'd be involving somebody else in the case unnecessarily, which would also take them away from their own work. But I do think we should have a chat with Jon Hall and tell him to keep an eye on who Longhorn's been communicating with over the past couple of days."

"All right. I'll agree to that. Do you think we should let the captain in on this?"

"He's testifying in court this morning, but we'll fill him in when he gets back. In the meantime, we certainly have some interesting new angles to work this from."

"That's for sure," Jordan said. "I think instead of focusing on luck rituals, I'm going to focus on Stonehenge."

"And while you're doing that, I'm going to research knives, the weather and photography."

"Interesting choices..." Jordan said, letting the end of his statement trail off. It was clear that he wanted an explanation.

"I had a brainwave last night just like you and Charles. I figure, this guy sure goes through a lot of knives if he leaves one sitting in the victim every time he kills. Either he buys them all—which might seem a little suspicious—or he knows how to make them himself."

"Maybe that's why he moved to Connecticut. Because I'm sure that over in New York anybody buying long sharp knives is causing suspicion and concern."

"I thought you were of the opinion that the guy liked causing suspicion."

"But not so much suspicion that it prevents him from being able to kill whenever he pleases," Jordan clarified. "Now what do the weather and photography have to do with anything?"

"Well I guess strictly speaking I'm not studying weather. More like the phases of the moon. Jack the Ripper supposedly killed according to them, why not this guy? Maybe it needs to be at just the right phase to cast the perfect shadow. It would go with the whole ritualistic thing. Photography comes into it as well because of the light and shadow. Most serial killers keep some kind of trophy, something that lets them go back and relive the crime again and again years later. But this guy doesn't seem to take anything. So maybe he just snaps a photo instead."

"He takes their cell phones," Jordan said. "Or at least we think he does. Maybe he takes a photo and an audio recording."

"I hadn't thought of that," Braxton replied. "But if he decides to turn the cell phone on to look or listen or whatever, then we should be able to trace it. Maybe we should let Jon Hall know about that as well when we talk to him about Charles."

"Good idea," Jordan said. "Getting back to the whole photography thing, though, what if the exact phase of the moon doesn't matter? So our guy isn't exactly like Jack the Ripper. He—Jack, that is—only killed his victims when the moon was on the same phase. But what if the shadow caused by the moon isn't exactly the same for all the victims? Let's say you're right about the photography thing and he has a bunch of photos of his handiwork stashed away somewhere."

"With you so far."

"I wonder what would happen if you placed all of those photos side by side in a line? Maybe he's trying to form some larger image with the way the shadows are."

"That's an idea," Braxton said, scribbling it down on the first random scrap of paper his hand touched. "Maybe that's how he chooses his victims, by which one would fit best in his line of pictures. But it still doesn't explain the change in location."

"Unless the backgrounds have some sort of significance as well. Maybe they all match up together to form a bigger picture. And he couldn't kill them all in the same place anyway; it would definitely look suspicious if two victims showed up in the same spot."

"Looks like we've both got a lot of work to do," Braxton said with a sigh. But it was invigorating to finally have a clear direction to go in, so they both set to work eagerly.

Chapter 9

DETECTIVE JORDAN QUICKLY discovered that Longhorn hadn't been kidding when he said there was a wide variety of theories about why Stonehenge had been built. Some of them—such as alien involvement—could be discarded without a second glance. But for other theories it was harder to tell one way or the other.

The statistics that Jordan found about the ancient monument were mind-boggling. It seemed to be a pretty widely accepted fact that the materials were floated down channels that had once existed on the Salisbury plains. They were then hoisted up using a system of ropes and pulleys. All of the engineering stuff was fascinating, but unfortunately it wasn't relevant at all to Jordan's investigation. Everybody (with the exception of a few conspiracy theorists) agreed on the *how* of Stonehenge. It was the question of *why* that spawned the most disagreement, and that was what Jordan spent the majority of his time looking into.

Jordan focused most of his energy on researching the theories that involved the Druids, an ancient Celtic group regarded as either revered prophets or feared outsiders, depending on who the author of the article was. Those who thought the Druids were prophets respected them for their groundbreaking ideas. Those who considered them outsiders respected them because they feared that not doing so would cause the Druids to kill one of their family members, or steal some of the cattle from their fields under cover of darkness.

One of the most interesting and terrifying things that Detective Jordan discovered during the course of his research that morning was that the Druids were known to offer sacrifices, both animal and—on occasion—human. There were plenty of documented accounts of animal sacrifice, which normally wouldn't seem all that alarming; many religions still participated in that particular practice even today. But since he was investigating a serial killer who might be getting ideas from the Druids, Jordan found the idea of any kind of sacrifices disturbing.

Most of the evidence for human sacrifice was in the form of stories, passed down from generation to generation and distorted God only knew how much from the original tale.

"Yes, my great-grandfather remembered well the night," most of these stories began. "It was dark and stormy. There was a bang outside so my great-grandfather and his brother went to make sure the gate for the corral hadn't come open; they didn't want any of the cattle getting loose. That was the last time he ever saw his brother again."

Invariably the stories would end with a sighting of lights coming from the direction of Stonehenge, almost as though a fire were burning. These lights were generally accompanied by strange noises. The obvious conclusion—well, obvious to the storytellers' minds anyway—was that there was a human sacrifice taking place, and the strange noises were the Druid priests and priestesses performing a dark ceremonial act. In other words, Stonehenge was a collection of stone altars used for evil purposes.

Surprisingly, Jordan also found some connection between the Druids and the theory that Stonehenge was used as an almanac for farmers. Many ancient Celtic religious holidays had been based off of the cycle of the sun. This fact was true for many systems of mythology but in the Druid system, solstices and equinoxes had special significance. These were the days when the barrier between the spirit world and the world of the living was thought to thin considerably, possibly even to the point of being able to cross realms. But this could not be done without performing a great sacrifice.

Braxton had an equally busy morning, measuring what the phases of the moon were on the days that the different murders took place, and also trying to determine how the moon might have looked from the various crime scenes. He also looked into Jack the Ripper and all the theories about him and why he had killed only at one certain phase of the moon. Similar to his partner, some of the theories that Braxton encountered were complete garbage. He didn't think it remotely possible, for example, that Jack the Ripper was a werewolf, or some other supernatural being that only got its power during the full moon. An unfortunate fact that Braxton had learned from his years on the police force was that there was enough human evil to deal with in the world without adding the supernatural into the mix as well.

They both took a break from their research at about mid-day to get a bite to eat. As they were eating, Braxton said, "I think we should talk to Shannon's family. We can try and see if she has any sort of connection to the other victims."

"Sounds like a good idea to me, I guess," said Jordan. He knew that Mr. and Mrs. O'Neal had been informed of their daughter's death last night, and he hated having to add to their misery by pressing them for small details. He knew that if (God forbid) something ever happened to Kaitlin, he wouldn't want somebody doing that to him. But if it would help them get a dangerous man off the streets, then he knew they had to do it. The interview went much the same as with all the other victims' families.

"Did you notice anyone giving Shannon any sort of undue attention?" Braxton asked.

"No," answered Mr. O'Neal. "She seemed perfectly happy when we talked to her earlier that day."

"When did you speak to her?" asked Jordan.

"About four o'clock that afternoon. She called us and said that she might be home a little bit late, but not to worry. She said she would just be over at her friend's house, studying for a chemistry test."

When she didn't come home for dinner and didn't pick up her cell phone, I called the friend she had supposedly been studying with," said Mrs. O'Neal, speaking up for the first time. "But she told me that Shannon hadn't been over that day, and they didn't even have a chemistry class together. I should have known that! What kind of mother doesn't know what classes their child is taking? She was telling me that to give me a clue that something was wrong, and if I had figured it out sooner, maybe she would still be alive."

And she hid her face in her handkerchief once more.

"Mrs. O'Neal, there was nothing you could have done. This wasn't your fault," Jordan said, trying to be comforting.

The two detectives glanced at one another and then Braxton said, "Thank you very much for your help. We won't take any more of your time."

"Please find whoever did this," Mrs. O'Neal said as the detectives got up to leave. "Find them so they won't hurt anyone else."

"I promise you we will," said Jordan. Braxton frowned at him but waited until they were safely back in their car to voice any objection.

"Just as a general warning, you shouldn't make promises that you might not be able to keep."

"You're doubting our ability to solve this case?"

"No. I'm doubting your ability to be realistic about things. You know as well as I do that the longer this investigation drags on, the less likely it is that we're going to be successful."

"What was I supposed to say?" Jordan lashed back. " 'We'll try our best but no guarantees'? That's not exactly a way to instill confidence in somebody."

"But I've never heard those words come out of your mouth in all the years we've worked together, and people still seem to believe in you, in us. Why are you so close to this?"

"You know why," Jordan yelled. He rarely raised his voice to his partner, but all the stress and pressure building up was about to break him if he didn't get some of it out. "The last crime scene was four blocks away from my house! Kaitlin walks that way to school every day. That could so easily have been her."

"But it wasn't," said Braxton. "It wasn't Kaitlin, and nothing is going to happen to her. Because I'm going to help you keep the promise you just made. We'll catch this guy."

Nothing more was said as they made their way back to the police station to continue their research.

"Sorry," Jordan said abruptly as they went inside and made their way upstairs.

"Don't be," said Braxton. "It's a tough case. But we're in it together, so you don't have to go through all this alone. Now let's get to work on keeping that promise."

Chapter 10

JUST AFTER THEY got back from talking with Shannon's family, Longhorn arrived carrying a huge stack of reference books about Irish mythology.

"Not all of this stuff is going to be relevant," he said, setting down his heavy load with a thump on the corner of Jordan's desk. "But I thought it would be a good idea to bring it all just in case."

"Thanks, Charles. This helps a lot. I've found some stuff on the Internet, but I think I trust books more. Call me old fashioned, but it's true."

"I'm the same way," Longhorn agreed.

Jordan eagerly started thumbing through the volumes that Longhorn had brought, but he didn't get very far before Braxton interrupted.

"If you've got a minute, Charles, maybe we could go over what we've come up with? Three heads are better than two. Maybe something we say will strike a chord with you and remind you of one of the other cases."

"Sure, I've got a minute. I'll have to duck out before too long, though; Levi Washington has a little break before the next newscast, so you never know if he might decide to get into trouble."

"You can have the spotlight first then," Braxton said courteously. Longhorn pulled around an extra rolling chair and settled himself in.

"I didn't really find out very much," Longhorn said, sounding disappointed. "I did get the case files though, and I printed out transcripts of all the newscasts that mentioned the Knifer. If the source of the leak is the same, then maybe they only have access to certain types of information."

"You think they're a record keeper of some kind. Or they work in an evidence lab?"

"Possibly. And that brings me to a question that I had for you two: does your forensics lab use any outside sources to do their testing?"

"I don't think so," said Braxton, "but let me check just to be sure."

While Braxton got on the phone, Jordan picked up one of Longhorn's books again. He flipped to the index page and looked under the letter *D*.

"D for what?" Longhorn asked, catching sight of what he was doing.

"Druid," Jordan answered. "They seemed like the right kind of people to base a ritualistic killing style off of."

"Ah, Druids," said Longhorn, with a reminiscent little sigh. He leaned back and closed his eyes. "My grandfather was full-blooded Irish. He used to tell me stories that he heard from his grandfather about the Druids."

"Let me guess: they all started out with 'My grandfather remembered well the night.'"

"Something like that," Longhorn agreed. "How did you guess?"

"I read a lot of stories online this morning and that was how quite a few of them started. You have to wonder how accurate those tales are though, being passed on from generation to generation like that."

At that point their conversation was cut off by a clunking noise as Braxton hung up the phone.

"No outside labs used for anything," he reported. "But they did give me the name of the place that they would send stuff to get DNA testing if there was anything to send."

Longhorn took the piece of paper that Braxton offered him; it had the name of the lab scribbled on it. "Not the same one we use," Longhorn said, shaking his head. "At least that might have given us a clue."

"There is one source we have in common," said Jordan. "We've both used Jonathan Hall."

"We—that is to say, those of us at the NYPD—have been very guarded with him, though. Never revealed any more information about the case than was strictly necessary. I'm sure the two of you did the same."

"Of course," Braxton replied. "But he would have the skills to get information he's not supposed to have."

"I just don't see him as being the media leak, though," said Longhorn. "The news didn't start picking up information until the third case, and Jon offered to help us right from the first case. Why would he wait?"

"To avoid suspicion?" Jordan suggested.

"It's possible I guess," said Longhorn.

"It's also possible that a police officer is the source of the leak," said Braxton. And he added pointedly, "A police officer who has been involved in all of the cases."

It was only with a great effort that Jordan contained his frustration. Braxton really wanted to confront Longhorn now, based on nothing but a gut feeling? They should be putting their heads together looking at the actual concrete evidence they had. Then again, maybe it was best for his partner to get this off his chest.

"I didn't have you pegged as a coward, Detective Braxton," said Longhorn coldly, his arms crossed over his chest.

"That's because I'm not."

"If you weren't, you would actually have the guts to say it to me directly: you think I'm the media leak. And let me guess, I'm probably the killer, too?"

"Yes to the first one, definitely. I'm less sure on the second one."

"I say 'no' to both of them," Jordan put in quietly.

"Okay. Let's get a few things straight. When would I have gotten the opportunity to spread information to Levi Washington and the other newsies in New York? Answer: I didn't have an opportunity, or a motive. I was a bit too busy trying to actually catch the man responsible for these horrible crimes. And, like you, I was against the idea of putting out a media hotline because it would excite the killer and it would be an invasion of the grieving families' privacy."

"You did have opportunity," Braxton pointed out. "Who knows what you were doing when you were supposed to be tailing Levi Washington? Or when you were driving back to New York today? And surely your boys from New York haven't been with you every moment of the day while you've been trying to track this guy down."

"You still can't explain the motive, can you?" Longhorn said. "Because—I repeat—there is no motive. My entire career I've been suspicious of using the news as a possible way to gather information, you can ask my captain or anyone on my squad if you don't believe me."

"Okay," said Braxton abruptly. "Let's say you're not the media leak. Who's to say you aren't the killer?"

"I was having dinner with my wife when the first Connecticut murder occurred. And I was sleeping on your couch at the time of the second one."

"Actually you were out tailing Levi Washington—alone, I might add—at the approximate time of death for our victim. So you could have done the deed then, stashed the body somewhere, and snuck out to dump it after we got to my place and I fell asleep."

"I think you're forgetting that you griped about me waking you up as I tiptoed to the restroom last night. If you heard that, I'm sure you would have heard someone sneaking out of and then back into your house."

At that, Jordan had to fight back a laugh. His partner was often known to complain about how every little noise he heard would wake him up during the night.

"Shut up, Mark," Braxton snapped at him.

"Sorry. But you are a light sleeper. And Longhorn has an alibi for Sarah Abernathy's murder. So, logically, he can't be our killer."

"All right, then," said Braxton, grudgingly. "Things just weren't quite adding up so I had to be sure, you know? And it made so much sense that the same person who spread the story over here in Connecticut was the same person that did so in New York. And I still think it's likely that the source and the killer are the same person."

"That much I agree with. But that person is not me. And there could be two different leaks, one in each state. I mean there's certainly more than one person that has some kind of grudge against the police and would want to cause trouble for them."

"There's also the possibility that there's more than one killer like you suggested to begin with, Mark," Braxton chimed in.

"The more I think about this, though, the more I think it's unlikely that two people are involved," Jordan replied. "If I'm right in thinking that this guy is basing his killings off of the ancient Druids, then he's probably a solo act. All the research I found has suggested that there were many different priests and priestesses but only one leader. This leader was the one responsible for choosing the perfect sacrificial victim. I think our killer sees himself as that lead priest. It's all up to him. It's a lot of responsibility, sure—but it also means that he's the one to get all the glory. And I think it's that possibility of fame—or infamy I guess might be a better way to put it—that ultimately drives him to do what he does."

"That could be what made him move states," Longhorn said. He still didn't quite look at Braxton, but addressed Jordan instead.

"That's what we were thinking. He wanted to spread his name around a little more."

"I think the real reason he moved was because the moon was better," Braxton put in, trying to transition the conversation toward what he had discovered in his own research throughout that day. It could not have been clearer that it was very difficult to hold in whatever news he had to share.

"What makes you think that, Steve?" Detective Jordan asked. He really was interested to hear what his partner had to say, but he knew better than to let that show through in his voice; it was best not to encourage Braxton's theatrical side too much.

"Maybe the Knifer was taking influence from both the Druids and from Jack the Ripper. I've read several crazy rumors about old Jack today, but one of them actually makes a little bit of sense: that the phases of the moon played a role in when the killings took place."

He paused for dramatic effect but neither Longhorn nor Jordan said anything so the effect was ruined slightly.

"Through the wonder of technology," Braxton continued after a moment, "I was able to look up what phase the moon was in on the date of each killing. Unfortunately the phases were all different, with the exception of two that were the same."

"Which two?" Jordan inquired.

"Victims 2 and 6. Why do you ask?"

"I just thought it might be significant if the two identical moon phases were also the two victims that went to the same school. Like maybe something made those two special, tied them together somehow. Guess not, though."

"The most recent victim never even attended school in New York, so the fact that all the other victims lived in New York might have been just a coincidence," Longhorn pointed out.

"Yes, it might be," Braxton said impatiently. "But you haven't even let me get to the good part yet."

"Sorry," Longhorn muttered, but he and Jordan exchanged furtive grins when Braxton wasn't looking.

"Thank you. Anyway, like I was saying I was initially disappointed that the phases of the moon weren't the same for all the crimes. But then I switched gears a bit and started looking at different types of photography, particularly nighttime photography. A big part of the tips that I found focused on which phases of the moon give the best light."

"Let me guess: the phases the tips listed were all the phases that the moon was in on the nights of the different murders," Jordan said.

"Yes," Braxton answered, smacking his pen on the table just to drive the point home. "Although frankly it would have been more dramatic if you had let me say that line."

"Is he always like this?" Longhorn asked. He was barely holding back laughter.

"Yes," Jordan said, also laughing. "You get used to it after a while."

He turned back to his partner and said, "All joking aside, that is a good idea. I'll add photography to the list of possible personality traits our killer has."

"And now that we have the original photos from all of the crime scenes, we can see if there are different shadows," Longhorn said. He produced the photographs from a briefcase that he was carrying and Braxton cleared off a free space on his desk so they could spread out all the photos and look at them.

"Every other victim is facing a different way than the others," Jordan pointed out after they had all stared at the photos for a minute. "The bodies of the odd numbered victims are straight and the bodies of the even numbered ones are sort of angled."

"But at opposite angles to each other," Braxton added.

"I'm not seeing any patterns jumping out at me," Longhorn said.

"Me neither," said Braxton. "Maybe we just need to think outside the box."

"That's it!" Jordan shouted, after a moment of silence.

Several of the other detectives that were in the room jumped at the sudden noise, but Detective Jordan ignored everyone else around him and launched himself at one of the pages of notes he had printed out.

Chapter II

BRAXTON AND LONGHORN both stared at Jordan in a rather bemused sort of way, wondering what he was searching for.

"You know, when you solve a case it's generally considered traditional to shout 'Eureka,'" Detective Lynch, who was sitting near them, pointed out. "Am I going to be hearing that from this table soon?"

"Maybe not," said Jordan, still flipping through his notes. "But I think we're about as close to a major breakthrough in this case as we've been since the NYPD started looking for him."

Jordan found what he was looking for at last, and held the sheet of paper close to his face, scrutinizing it.

"Gonna let us in on that breakthrough?" Braxton asked, raising his eyebrows.

"You're the one that gave it to me," Jordan said. "We need to think outside the box. We've been looking at these pictures in a line, but what if they're in a circle?"

As he spoke he started rearranging the pictures, setting them a certain distance apart. Every now and then he double-checked the sheet he was holding. After a minute or two, he stepped back. With the way the pictures were arranged now, all the shadows cast by the knives, and by the bodies of the victims themselves, pointed to the same central location in the middle of the circle. There were also little sections of light in between the shadows, like the spokes on a bicycle tire.

"Why did you leave this space blank?" Longhorn asked, indicating a large gap between the last picture and the first. The arrangement on the table was more of a horseshoe than a circle.

"Because the pattern isn't complete. He's not done killing. I think—and again, this is all just a theory still, so I'm not one hundred percent sure—but I think he plans to kill one more person."

"Just one?" Braxton asked. The others stared at him, shocked to hear the happiness in his tone. "Well I mean of course I don't want him to kill anybody else! I was just asking, what makes you think he'll only kill one more person?"

"That's all it will take to complete the circle," Jordan said. "The circle of Stonehenge."

And he laid down the piece of paper he had been consulting with a dramatic flourish that more than matched his partner's. The paper was an aerial view of what Stonehenge looked like, and the outer ring was made up of seven stones, all angled in very particular ways.

"There was this one article that I found…where is it…ah, here it is," Jordan said, pulling out another sheet of paper from the pile on his desk. He read aloud, "'Stonehenge has seven stones in its outer ring. The placement of these stones is widely thought to have been decided based on what type of shadow the stones would cast when the light—cast by either the sun or the moon—struck them in a particular way. If the stones were not arranged in this particular fashion, the sun would not touch the heel stone on the summer solstice, thus ruining the use of Stonehenge as an almanac.'"

"But our guy isn't recreating an ancient almanac," Longhorn said dryly. "You can buy much more accurate ones in bookstores these days. Or just turn on your television."

"No, he isn't creating an almanac. I was getting to that part," Jordan said. He thought he understood now why Braxton didn't appreciate having his thunder stolen. "According to a different article I read, the stone in the very center of the circle was an altar of sorts that was used by the Druids in their ancient practices. There's some speculation that maybe the other layers of the ring were secondary altars, but that's not the point.

"The point is that the central stone was the one that was used for human sacrifices. And those sacrifices were performed on specific days of the year, when the border between this world and the spirit world was thin. And it was on those days that the moonlight cast the altar entirely in shadow."

"So there might be an eighth victim," Braxton said slowly.

"What do you mean?" Jordan asked.

"I mean, I agree with you that there's going to be a seventh victim to fill out the circle. But then who is the human sacrifice going to be?"

"Unless he plans on killing himself, surrounded by pictures of his victims?" Longhorn said. "That would even go along with Mark's idea about him being driven by fame. Sure, his body would be dead, but he would be going out with a bang."

"That means the act would take place in a very public area," Braxton said. "He'd want to be sure that as many people saw it as possible."

"I think we're getting a bit ahead of ourselves," said Jordan, frowning. "We still need to try and avoid there being a seventh victim instead of focusing on the eighth killing, if there's even going to be one. I mean honestly it wouldn't be such a great loss if he did kill himself, but we still want to bring him to justice."

"You're right," Braxton acknowledged. "Sorry. I guess I just got caught up in the excitement of actually having a breakthrough."

"Same goes for me," Longhorn agreed. "Do you have any thoughts about who the seventh victim might be?"

"I think it's a safe bet she'll be blond, like all the others," Jordan said. "What we really need to figure out is when the moon is going to be in the correct position to cast exactly the right shadow."

"I bet there's a software program that can do that," Braxton said.

"And I bet I know a guy that can tell us where to get our hands on it. Or, better yet, just do it himself and give us the information so we don't have to deal with a learning curve."

"Our friend Jonathan Hall," Braxton said, nodding. "You guys feeling up to a road trip?"

"Sure," said Jordan. "Let's go fill the captain in first, though."

Captain Huntington was very pleased to hear of the latest developments in the case. He was less pleased when they told him about their next plan of action.

"We've already agreed that Jonathan Hall is a common link between our two departments; to be more exact, he seems to be the only link. So I don't think we should be using him any more. Our own forensics lab can probably give us the same information. Or maybe the one up in New Haven, since it's bigger."

"Let's get going, then," said Longhorn, standing up.

"Actually, Charles, I still want you focused on the leak. Maybe he or she won't lead us to the killer, but we still need to be covering all our bases.

"Okay," said Longhorn. "Mark, Steve, keep me updated, will you?"

"You do the same," Braxton replied.

And with that, they all went their separate ways.

⭑⭑⭑

Once Jordan and Braxton had shown their credentials at the forensics lab and explained the reason they were there, the receptionist escorted them downstairs to a dimly lit room with computers ranged all around the walls. In fact, the setup looked eerily similar to Jon Hall's office. If the amount of complex equipment was anything to judge by, they had definitely come to the right place.

They explained their situation to a woman named Carolyn, who led them over to a computer and entered the information that they had provided. Then she scanned pictures of all the crime scenes into the computer and created an image on another screen with all of the pictures lined up in the way that Braxton and Jordan had specified.

"So all of the shadows have to point to the center?" Carolyn asked, just to clarify.

"Exactly," Braxton said.

Carolyn pressed a few keys and a little indistinct shape appeared in the gap that was left blank. Squinting, Jordan saw that this little shape was actually a miniature figure of a human being.

"We can adjust the size and position of this image until the shadow falls where it's supposed to be," Carolyn told them.

"So we just guess? The whole thing is trial and error?" Braxton asked.

"Oh no. The computer program makes all the adjustments, and then spits out the possible results; it should only take a few minutes." She hesitated and then asked, "This is for the case of the Knifer isn't it?"

Braxton and Jordan looked at each other briefly. There was no real use deny-ing it, given what the crime scene photos looked like.

"Yes," Jordan said with a sigh.

"However," Braxton added, picking up where his partner had left off, "we would like to take this opportunity to strongly remind you that any information you divulge to us today should remain strictly confidential. Is that understood?"

"I've been doing this job for a long time, Detective," said Carolyn, looking him straight in the eyes as she spoke. "I know about confidentiality. You can trust me not to tell anyone anything."

"Good," Braxton answered approvingly.

Just then the computer gave a series of three pings. With each ping an image popped up on the screen. Each image showed a human body in a slightly differ-ent position.

"OK," Carolyn said, turning her attention away from the two detectives and back to the computer screen in front of her. "So this program is saying that there are three possibilities for ways to convey that particular shadow."

"We can rule out the last one, don't you think, Mark?" said Braxton, point-ing to an image of a rather fat person lying on her side.

"Definitely," said Jordan. Carolyn did as they requested and then Jordan asked her, "Can you add in the figure of a knife sticking out from their chest?"

Carolyn made the requested adjustment and a rotating hourglass popped up: the computer was recalculating. There was a tense silence while they waited. To both of the detectives the wait seemed to drag on for hours, but it was really only a few minutes. When it was done, there was only one possibility.

Jordan stared at the completed circle in amazement.

"Fits the profile of the others, appearance wise I mean."

"Yeah," said Braxton.

"I can give you the exact height and approximate weight of your next vic-tim," said Carolyn.

The numbers popped up on the screen and Braxton recorded them dutifully in his notebook. Jordan could not say anything; he could only stare. The num-bers on the screen were very familiar.

"Forgive me if this sounds strange, but would you be able to determine what the moon and the weather would have to be like to cast that particular shadow?" Braxton asked.

"Not with this equipment," said Carolyn. "But I'll take you down the hall and introduce you to Ashley; she has the software you need."

Much as the two partners disliked having to bring in another person, they knew they had no choice, especially if it led to their solving this case and preventing the deaths of more people. So they followed Carolyn out of her lab and down to Ashley's.

Once they were there, Braxton asked his question again and Carolyn sent the image to Ashley's computer. Ashley then entered a bit of information, and while they were waiting for the results, she pulled up a nautical chart which showed upcoming phases of the moon, and a detailed satellite image of what the weather was supposed to be like. By the time she was finished with all of that, the computer had come up with two possible alternatives for casting the perfect shadow.

"If there was a full moon and a partly cloudy sky, that would work. Or there could be a moon that was three-quarters of the way full with not a cloud to be seen."

Braxton peered over her shoulder at the weather charts she had pulled up.

"You're not going to like this," said Jordan who was consulting the chart that depicted the upcoming phases of the moon. "There's a full moon tonight."

"And it's supposed to be perfectly clear without a cloud in the sky," Braxton said, sighing. "Perfect weather for stargazing. You're right, I don't like that."

"You've been very helpful, ma'am," said Detective Jordan. "But if you'll excuse us, we probably should be going."

Braxton frowned at him but followed his lead and left. He waited until they got to the car to ask what was wrong.

"The height and weight that you wrote down? That's Kaitlin's height and weight. Add in the fact that she's blond and about the same age as the other girls…" He took a deep breath and then admitted what it almost killed him to say.

"I think my daughter might be the Knifer's next target."

Chapter 12

CHARLES LONGHORN SAT in his car, staring fruitlessly up at the news station building and trying not to dwell on the confrontation that had just taken place. He hadn't revealed anything in front of Captain Huntington, but he had been deeply hurt and angered by Braxton's insinuation that he was the killer. His reasons for being suspicious of Longhorn as the leak had almost made sense, but as the killer? Longhorn knew he was innocent, but it seemed like the only way to prove that to Braxton beyond any doubt was to catch the actual murderer.

And yet, here he was trying to catch an anonymous media tipster. The more he thought about it, the more frustrated he became. How could finding the media leak even help them find the killer, anyway? That was a long shot at the very best. It occurred to Longhorn that he could just leave; make a break back for New York while everyone was distracted. He doubted they would even miss him until the next body turned up. Longhorn had actually put his car in gear to act on this plan when his phone rang.

"Hello?" he answered, reluctantly putting his car in park again.

"Charles? This is Captain Huntington. I need you to come back to our precinct. We have a problem."

"What kind of problem? Please don't tell me it's another victim."

"It's not. But it's also a problem that's best discussed face to face instead of over the phone."

"I'm on my way," said Longhorn and hung up, still completely lost as to what the captain might be talking about. Braxton and Jordan arrived at about the same time that he did.

"I wonder what's going on," said Braxton as they walked inside.

"I wonder why the captain didn't want to discuss it over the phone," Longhorn added.

"I got a call from Jon Hall," the captain said when they had all made their way upstairs. "He said we should turn on the news."

And he moved slightly so they could see the TV screen behind him. A reporter was standing in front of the crime scene from the night before. Captain Huntington turned up the volume so they could hear what he was saying.

"Once again, we cannot legally reveal the name of the latest victim, due to her age. However, we do know that unlike the Knifer's other victims, this young woman lived in Connecticut, and not New York. It still remains unclear why the mysterious killer has moved, but Connecticut police are working with members of the NYPD to track him down. The only question that remains is will they be able to stop him before he kills again? Now back to you in the studio."

"How is that possible, how do they have that information?" Braxton burst out.

"That station manager has got some kind of nerve," Longhorn said at the same time.

"They must be one and the same," said Jordan. Somehow, his quiet voice was heard over the other two.

Longhorn, Braxton, and Huntington all fell silent and turned to stare at him.

"It's obvious isn't it?" said Jordan. "The only way Levi's source knows that information is if he was there. And the only person we know for a fact was there, is the killer."

"Or it could be someone from within one of our organizations," said Braxton.

"Don't start that again," Longhorn snapped.

"Don't start what again?" Huntington asked.

"Your detective here accused me of being Levi's source."

"Your captain thought you might be, too. That's why he sent you down here in the first place."

"And here I thought my input was actually valued," said Longhorn, after a brief pause to recover from the shock of this news.

"Of course it's valued. If you hadn't put us on the track of Irish mythology, we wouldn't be nearly as far along as we are," Jordan pointed out. "Besides, as long as we're agreed that the source and the killer are one and the same, it can't have been Longhorn. As I thought we had established earlier this afternoon."

And he glared at his partner until Braxton dropped his gaze.

"You're right," he finally said. "Charles, I'm sorry for suspecting you."

Longhorn only hesitated a moment before he took Braxton's outstretched hand.

"Apology accepted. Now I think we should move on to finding the real killer."

Before anyone could reply, Longhorn's cell phone rang. Seeing that it was Jonathan Hall calling, Longhorn put it on speaker so they could all hear.

"What is it, Jon?"

"I assume Neil told you to watch the news?"

"Yes, Captain Huntington did," said the captain.

"Oh, so you're there, too."

"Yes, and so are Detectives Jordan and Braxton, whom you met the other day. Now would you care to get on with your point?"

"Well, as soon as I saw the news report I took it upon myself to start searching around. An unregistered phone at the news station sent a blank text message earlier this morning. Five minutes later, the same phone received the only call it's ever gotten."

"Which would make sense if Levi ditched his cell phone and got a new one," said Longhorn. "Jon, could you tell where the call originated from?"

"It was too short for me to zero in on completely, but it was from somewhere within a square mile of the old warehouse district down at the opposite side of town from you guys."

Jordan caught his captain's eye and drew a hand across his throat. Huntington nodded and said, "Thanks for your help, Jon. We'll be in touch."

Longhorn hung up.

"Well, what are we waiting for? Let's go."

"If this is a wild goose chase, which it almost certainly is, then we don't have time for it," said Jordan.

"And why is that?"

"Because the next murder—and, if Mark is right, the last murder—is going to happen tonight," Braxton answered.

"Well you got the height and weight of the next victim, right? We could go to the media ourselves, warn people who match that description to stay inside tonight."

"About that," said Jordan, and then stopped. He stared out the window for a minute, collecting himself, then looked back at his captain.

"Captain, those measurements we collected are my daughter's. They match her perfectly. As much as I would like to catch this guy, I think my place is with my family right now."

"We'll bring them here," said Captain Huntington. "On my life, Mark, your family will be kept safe. Why don't you go call them right now?"

Jordan left to do just that; it was not a call that he was looking forward to. As he had expected, Lisa was not at all happy when she received the news that Kaitlin could be a possible target for the Knifer. At first he thought—or maybe hoped—that the phone had dropped the connection, or that she hadn't heard him, because she didn't say anything. But then she regained her voice.

She raged at him for almost two full minutes before Jordan interrupted her.

"I only discovered this about half an hour ago, which is why I didn't tell you before."

"Then you should have called me half an hour ago!"

"I know, I'm sorry. The captain called and told us to get back to the station. Besides, I figured this conversation should be held in private, not with Steve sitting right beside me."

"So where are you right now?"

"I'm back at the precinct, and Captain Huntington wants you and Kaitlin here, too. Are you able to leave work and come down?"

"Of course. I'll pick up Kaitlin on my way. Should we tell her what's going on?"

Jordan had to think about that one for a minute.

"I think in this case ignorance would be bliss for her. She already knows that I've been working to try and catch the Knifer, but if she starts asking questions, just tell her I'm being overly protective."

"Okay," said Lisa.

"And tell her something else. Tell her I love her. She may not want to hear it, but it's the truth and she needs to know it."

"Of course she'll want to hear it," his wife assured him. "But it would sound a whole lot better coming directly from you. So yes, I'll tell her for you. But you can tell her yourself too when we see you at the station."

"All right," Jordan replied. "It's a promise. I'll see you soon, but I really have to go now. We may have a lead about where to find this guy—or someone who can lead us to him."

"Right. Goodbye, Mark. I love you so much."

"Love you, too. Goodbye," Jordan replied, and hung up. He could easily have stayed there saying goodbye all day, but he knew that wasn't an option. He walked back to Captain Huntington's office to see if the others had figured out some sort of action plan.

Chapter 13

THE PLAN THEY had devised was to send Longhorn, Braxton, Detective Lynch, and Detective Matthews down to the warehouse district. Then they would stage a call between Detective Alan Taylor and Levi Washington. Detective Taylor would pretend to be Levi's source, calling him with information that another murder would take place that night. Their hope was that Levi would realize the call wasn't actually from his source, call the real person, and Jon would be able to track the location and tell the detectives in the field exactly where to go. After all, one square mile was a large area for just four men to try and cover.

Now there was nothing to do but wait while the detectives in the field got into position. Jordan expected the wait to seem endless, but it actually passed rather quickly. Detective Jordan's biggest concern was that this was a very hastily thrown together plan. And he knew from experience that a lot could go wrong with a plan like that. Still, it was the best thing they could do, and it seemed like the only chance they had of finding a clue as to where the Knifer was hidden.

Before Jordan had too much time to dwell on the holes in their plan, he was sitting in one of the interview rooms with Detective Taylor and Captain Huntington. The room's phone was on a conference call so that everybody, including Jonathan, would be able to listen in to the conversation that was about to take place between Levi Washington and Alan Taylor.

"There should not be a sound unless it comes from the mouth of Detective Taylor," Captain Huntington reminded everyone in a stern voice. "Is that understood?"

"Yes, sir," came a chorus of voices.

"All right. Jon, you all set on your end?"

"Ready when you are, Neil—or I guess I should call you Captain Huntington since you're on the job."

"I don't care what you call me, as long as you get me access to that phone call. Detective Taylor, let's go."

"Dialing now."

There was a pause, followed by a loud clicking noise, and a dial tone like one used to hear on computers that used a phone line to connect to the Internet. Then Levi Washington's voice was heard.

"This is Levi. Who's calling, please?"

"You know who it is," Detective Taylor replied. He put just a hint of scorn in his voice, and he also put on a newscaster accent—the type that would fit in anywhere in America. It was subtle, and it didn't arouse any undue suspicion, but it also disguised his real voice.

"Hold on a second."

Dimly, they heard a door shut and lock.

"Okay, I'm in my office now," Levi informed them. A note of unmistakable greed came into his voice as he said, "We're just finalizing the lineup for today's news broadcast. Do you have a lead story for me like you promised?"

"Like he promised?" Jordan mouthed at his captain. In answer, Huntington frowned in concentration and put a finger to his lips, even though Jordan hadn't actually made a sound.

"Have I ever let you down all those times I've been in touch with you in the past?" Detective Taylor replied.

"Can't say that you have. Hold on a second, let me get some paper and a pen."

"Tell me when you're ready, but hurry up. I can't stay on the phone too long in case the cops try and trace it."

"I thought you said you knew how to cover your tracks."

"I do," said Taylor as though this were the most obvious fact in the world. "Why do you think I'm calling from a different phone number? But I still don't like taking chances."

"Make it quick then. What do you got?"

"A murder will take place tonight. And it will be the last."

"Where? You said you would tell me."

Taylor hesitated; he didn't know how to answer that. Then Huntington pointed at the badge he wore and nodded. Taylor got the message: the best thing to do would be to arouse a little suspicion. After all, it might make Levi more likely to actually call his source.

"If we knew that, this creep would be off the streets already, wouldn't he?"

There was silence for a few seconds, and then a loud click and a dial tone. Levi Washington had killed the connection.

"Well Jon?" Huntington demanded as soon as he was sure the connection to Levi had been dropped and he wouldn't be overheard. "Did it work?"

"Levi's making another call right now. I'll see if I can get you in. Just keep quiet, in case it turns out that he can hear us, too."

They all obeyed him, and listened to the sound of frantic typing on a keyboard.

"Got it."

And then all of them heard Levi Washington's voice again.

"It's me. Wherever you are, get out. The cops are on to you. I just got a call that I thought was from you. They don't know who you really are, though. But you're in danger. Please confirm somehow that you got this message. You know how to reach me."

"Where did it come from?"

"I can't tell you the exact location," Jonathan said. "The call ended too fast. But what I can tell you is that it didn't go to a phone that's anywhere near the warehouse district."

"What about the other phone call that you said did come from here?" Longhorn demanded.

"I guess he's on the move again. Probably stalking his next victim, if he plans to strike again soon."

"So we just wasted a whole lot of time for nothing," Braxton said.

"Well, thanks for your help, Jon," said Huntington. "And thank you as well, Detective Taylor. I know that couldn't have been an easy thing to do, and I appreciate you doing it on such short notice."

"No problem, captain. Glad I could help."

"Everyone at the warehouse site, come back to the precinct as fast as you can. We'll see you soon," said Huntington and then severed the connection.

"Well that was a bust," said Jordan, sounding disappointed and frustrated.

"Maybe not entirely," said Huntington; his face was grim, but there was a flicker of triumph in his eyes.

Before Jordan could ask what he meant, one of their new recruits pulled open the door, looking extremely nervous.

"What is it?" Huntington asked. But the detective addressed Detective Jordan instead.

"Sir, your wife just arrived to see you. Is there something wrong?" he added, noticing the puzzled look on Jordan's face.

"I guess I'd better go find out," Jordan answered. "Where is she?"

"In the captain's office; she seemed upset, so I thought it would be best to give her some privacy."

"Thank you," said Detective Jordan. His voice might have been calm but his heart was racing. Why had the officer not mentioned Kaitlin? He walked quickly down the hall towards Huntington's office, with the captain right behind him.

"Would you like someone to go in there with you?" asked the captain as they stood outside the closed door to his office.

"I'd appreciate a moment alone, actually. I think this is something that needs to happen between just the two of us."

The captain nodded and stood aside.

The moment Jordan entered the room his wife fell into his chest, crying hysterically. Judging by how red her eyes and cheeks were, she had been crying for quite some time. And it took a few minutes of Jordan just holding her and rocking her gently back and forth for the tears to stop, or at least die down to the point where Lisa was capable of coherent speech.

"Come sit down," Jordan said gently. He pushed her down into one of the chairs that Captain Huntington had in front of his desk. Then he sat down beside her.

"Tell me what's wrong, Lisa."

But he thought he might already know.

She dabbed at her eyes a moment longer and then looked up at him.

"It's K-Kaitlin. She's gone. I went to pull her out of rehearsal early and bring her here, like you said, but I was the only one there.

"What do you mean?"

"The director has the flu apparently, so he told all the cast members to head home. There was a note taped to the door."

"So Kaitlin would have found out right after she got out of school. More than enough time for her to get home," Jordan muttered. He was forced to accept the truth: his daughter had been kidnapped, and in all likelihood she would end up being the next victim of the mysterious Knifer.

"You don't think…I mean even if she has been kidnapped and singled out, he wouldn't kill her would he? Not this soon? I mean, there's been space between all the other murders." His wife's eyes clearly communicated that she needed some kind of hope. But at that moment Jordan decided that honesty was a better policy than making promises he wasn't sure that he could keep.

"We know—or we think we know—when the next crime is going to take place. And that's tonight."

"Tonight? But he's been successfully avoiding those cops in New York for three months."

"Those cops in New York aren't as intuitive as your husband is," said Detective Longhorn from the doorway, exaggerating his already thick New York accent; he and the others had just arrived back from the warehouse district. "His investigative skills truly are impressive. Thanks to him and his partner, we know a whole lot about this killer. We still don't have an exact identity, but we're getting close."

"You might be wrong there, Detective," said Huntington quietly. "I think I know who the Knifer is."

Chapter 14

"SO WHEN EXACTLY did you come to this conclusion?" Jordan asked. Longhorn's eyes echoed the question.

"I can't say. Not with Lisa in the room."

"Come on, captain. She's involved in this now. She might as well be updated on the progress of the investigation. Isn't that her right?"

"Technically, I should also remove you from this case."

"You wouldn't do that, would you, Neil?" Lisa asked, her eyes huge and red-rimmed. "My husband is the person I trust most to solve this. No offense to the rest of you, of course. Besides, he has even more motivation now."

"Your husband might have too much motivation. It's what we call in the police business a conflict of interest."

"With all due respect, sir, my wife is right. There isn't a chance on this Earth that you can force me off this case, not when my daughter's life may be in jeopardy. And if you do take me off of the case, then I should remind you that my free time is mine to spend how I choose."

Captain Huntington stared at him, and Jordan did not look away. So Huntington had no choice but to go against his better judgment.

"Fine," he said. "You can stay on the case. But if you slip up, or it looks like you might slip up, you're off of it. I will handcuff you to that desk if it turns out that that's what's necessary. Do I make myself very clear?"

"Yes, sir."

"Good. But I still can't say anything in front of Lisa. I'm sorry. But that's the law."

"Maybe you should go, honey," Jordan said, turning to his wife and rubbing her shoulders. "Why don't you sit at my desk and wait? I'll walk you out there."

Lisa got up and the two of them exited the office. As soon as the door had closed behind them, Braxton spoke up.

"Are you sure this is a good idea, captain? Letting Mark stay on this case."

"You've worked with him a lot more closely than I have," Huntington replied. "Do you trust that he will be able to handle this?"

"Without a doubt," said Braxton.

"Then it is the best idea. But I expect you to keep a close watch on him just in case."

"Understood."

That was all the conversation they had time for before Detective Jordan walked back into the room.

"Sit down," said Huntington. "Steve, could you grab another chair for us please?"

"I'd prefer to stand, actually," Jordan said. His voice was polite, but it was quivering with tension. He appeared to notice this himself so he closed his eyes and took a few slow, calming breaths. Then he added, "Besides, worrying about chairs seems a bit of a waste of time when you told us you think you know who the killer is."

Everyone except Detective Jordan sat down, and Captain Huntington seemed ready to speak at last.

"It seems fairly plain that the killer and the source of the media leak are the same person. It also seems fairly plain that Levi Washington knew this."

"With you so far," said Jordan; he really wished his captain would get to the point already. The questions that Washington had been asking, unashamedly fishing for information, suggested the two obvious points that Huntington had just suggested.

"I believe the man we're looking for is none other than Jonathan Hall."

Dead silence in the room.

"Well now I'm not with you," Braxton said bluntly after a moment to catch his breath following this bombshell.

"There are several points which back up my suspicions," Huntington said. "Firstly, I understand that the NYPD has made use of his services throughout this investigation?"

"Yes," Longhorn confirmed. And then his eyes got a little wider as he had a revelation. "In fact he was the one who offered his skills. And he did so right from the very first case, before we even knew that we were dealing with a serial killer."

"And it's not unusual for killers to insert themselves into the investigation soon after it starts," Braxton added, picking up where Longhorn left off. "That way they can keep track of what sort of progress the police are making toward catching him or her."

"And they can decide when and where it's safe to kill again," said Longhorn. "They could lead the police on a wild goose chase if they wanted to."

"That sounds familiar, doesn't it?" asked Captain Huntington rhetorically. "It seems pretty plain now that there was never any killer or media leak hiding out in the warehouse district."

Everything Huntington was saying made perfect logical sense, but Jordan wasn't quite ready to believe Hall was guilty. How could all of them have committed that large and that serious of an oversight?

"On the other hand," he said now, "what if Jon Hall is just a nice guy? He saw an opportunity to help, so he took it."

"It is a possibility," Huntington acknowledged. "But you also have to understand that Jon was in a unique position to lead the police on a wild goose chase, as Detective Longhorn phrased it just now. There's a distinct lack of physical evidence with these crimes; everything we've been relying on has come from technology—tracing phone calls, for example."

"You think he tampered with the evidence?" Braxton asked. Unlike his partner, he fully accepted that Jonathan Hall was actually the Knifer.

"He certainly could have," the captain replied.

"Wait a minute..." Longhorn said, and then stopped. He appeared to be thinking very hard. "Sir, can you place a call to the forensics lab that you use? Specifically the department that has to do with tracing phone calls?"

Captain Huntington, after flipping through a Rolodex on his desk, dialed the number and requested to be transferred to the correct department. He put the phone on speaker so that everyone could listen in on the conversation.

"How can I help you?" asked a bright, chirping little voice.

"I need to know the answer to one question," Longhorn said. "If a call was placed from a payphone, would it be possible to trace the location of whatever phone received the call?"

"That depends," said the woman on the phone. "How long did the call last?"

"Two minutes or so?" Longhorn said. "I don't have the exact time in front of me at the moment."

"You're sure it was over a minute and fifteen seconds, though?"

"Yes. Definitely."

"Then that's plenty of time to trace a call."

"Would it matter if you tried to trace the call after the person calling had already hung up?"

"Not in the slightest. I mean, the location wouldn't be quite as accurate, but you would still be able to trace it to within a few square miles or so."

"Do you mind if I put you on hold for just one moment please?"

"Not a problem."

"Thanks," said Longhorn, and gestured for Captain Huntington, who was nearest the phone, to press the hold button.

"What was that all about?" Jordan asked.

"The first night I started watching Levi Washington, after I interviewed him? He made a call from a payphone. As soon as I saw him making it, I called Jon Hall for his help. But he didn't answer his phone until after Levi walked away. When I asked him why he said it was because he was on a call with somebody else.

"If it's all right by you, Captain, I'd like to ask the woman from your lab to trace what number Levi's call was placed to. I don't even care about the location, but if it's Hall's number..."

"Good plan," Huntington said approvingly. He took the phone off hold. "If we give you the time a call was placed and the location of the payphone where it was made, could you tell us the number of the phone that received the call?"

"Sure. Give me just a second." There was about half a minute's silence and the sound of a mouse clicking a few times and then she said, "Okay, where was the payphone?"

Longhorn consulted his notes and gave the forensic technician all the information that she asked for.

"Ready for your answer?" she asked after a few moments of silence.

"Go ahead," said Longhorn.

"914-624-2273."

Silence fell in the room. Everyone present knew that the number the technician had just read off belonged to Jonathan Hall.

"Bad news I take it?" the woman on the phone asked, somewhat hesitantly.

"Bad news is better than no news," said Huntington. "What's your name?"

"Alicia," answered the forensic tech.

"Would you be willing to testify in a courtroom that you performed this search and arrived at this conclusion?"

"If it helps to put a criminal behind bars then yes," Alicia said. "I'd be happy to help in whatever way I can."

"Thank you very much. We might be back in touch with you soon."

Everyone in the room now focused their attention on Detective Jordan. The evidence against Jon Hall was quickly piling up, and they wanted to see how he would react to that. He had to admit, it was hard to overlook.

"I just don't know why he would do something like this," said Jordan. "What if someone's framing him?" He knew he was reaching but he couldn't help it.

"I don't think that's the case, Mark," said Huntington. His voice was sympathetic, but still remained calm and logical. "You'll recall what he said when he was talking about that call that supposedly came from the warehouse?"

Jordan shook his head; he had too much on his mind to remember details as specific as that.

"He said, 'He's probably stalking his next victim if he's planning to strike again soon.' Did any of us tell him we were trying to listen in to the killer?"

"When I called and asked for his help, I didn't say anything about who we were trying to track down," said Braxton. "I just said we needed to listen in on a phone conversation."

"I would hazard a guess that the call Levi got earlier today—the one where the source told him to expect another call—came from Jonathan Hall's phone. We could confirm that theory by calling our friend Alicia again."

"No. Don't waste time doing that," said Jordan. "I think our talents would be put to better use in finding Jon. And Kaitlin."

The rest of them had no idea how difficult it was for Jordan to say that, to admit that he had made a mistake and missed some critical clue that would have enabled him to save his daughter.

But his daughter wasn't dead yet. And if Jordan had anything to say about it, she would not die at the hands of the Knifer.

Chapter 15

"Under other circumstances I would suggest that the best course of action would be to just call Jon and set up a time to meet with him; we could pretend we knew nothing," said Captain Huntington.

"And why is that not a viable solution in this case?" Jordan asked him. He stood with his arms folded tightly over his chest but now that they were actually discussing something to do, he felt a little bit of the tension leaving his body.

"Because he's smart. And because he was on that phone call with us, he knew we were getting close to finding him."

"But that's one thing I don't get," Longhorn said. "Why would he put us in on Levi's second call if he knew we would be led right back to him?"

"My guess is that he thought we weren't smart enough to figure it out," said Braxton. "Maybe we deserved that low opinion he gave us. After all, we welcomed him into this investigation with open arms."

"He also might have thought that it would look even more suspicious if he suddenly refused to help us after offering his services in the first place," Jordan pointed out.

"I wonder how long he's been planning something like this," murmured the police captain. "I got to know him a long time ago. But maybe the whole time we've been acquainted he's just been trying to use the relationship he has with me as an excuse for being able to keep a close eye on the police without arousing any undue suspicion. Mark, did Jon know that you had a daughter?"

Jordan closed his eyes and rubbed his hands over his face, forcing himself to look back and remember and think. Had he ever mentioned Kaitlin in conversation?

"I don't think so," he said out loud after a minute. "Steve, do you remember anything I don't?"

"No, you never mentioned her," Braxton answered, after wracking his own brains. "But he's a computer genius. He could easily have looked it up. Come to think of it, that's what I would do if I were a serial killer with his particular brand of skills. I would find out everything I could about my enemy."

"If he knows about Kaitlin then he knows about Lisa," Jordan said.

"All the more reason to keep her here where she's safe," said Captain Huntington. "You can trust us to look after her, Detective."

"If her life can't be in my hands then I'm glad it's in yours, Captain."

"I think the best thing we can do in this case is to split up," said Huntington. "Two people will go to Jon's office in New York. We'll see if we can get in touch with some of our own computer gurus and have them track his phone, give us accurate information. Although he's probably turned his phone off, if he thinks there's even a chance that we're on to him."

"I'll go," said Longhorn. "I'd like to be there when he's arrested if it's all the same to you."

"I'll go, too," said Jordan. "For the same reason."

"No, you won't," Huntington replied, his voice kind but also firm; it was immediately clear that no amount of arguing would yield any sort of result. "Longhorn, I'm not your captain, so I acknowledge that I have no authority whatsoever over you. But you're not going alone. Take Detective Lynch. Don't leave just yet, though," he added, as Longhorn and Lynch made for the door. "We need to discuss the rest of the plan."

"I assume that includes telling me where I'll be instead of tracking down my daughter's kidnapper?" Jordan asked.

"Yes," the captain replied, "And you would do well to watch your tone. You and your partner will be retracing Kaitlin's footsteps. Find out where she went, if she was with anyone, or if there is any chance at all that someone might have seen her get taken."

"Yes, sir," said Detective Jordan. As much as he longed to be there to witness Jon Hall getting arrested, he had to acknowledge the sense in the captain's plan; he knew his daughter's habits best, and therefore had the best chance on picking up on something that was out of the ordinary.

Now that Jordan had received his assignment he was eager to get going. This must have shown in his face—or possibly in the way that he was hopping back and forth from foot to foot as though he were dancing on hot coals. So Captain Huntington called an end to their meeting and told everyone to go about the tasks assigned to them.

"And I want updates every half hour from both teams, is that understood?"

"Yes, sir," they all replied.

Longhorn and Detective Lynch left first, and Detectives Jordan and Braxton left soon afterward, but not before Jordan stopped to talk with his wife about what the plan was. He didn't give her specifics, but he told her enough to assure her.

"I have to call in and report to Captain Huntington every thirty minutes. So every half an hour you'll know for certain that I'm safe. He said you can sit in his office if you'd like, now that we're done talking about things in there."

"Make sure you call on time," Lisa told him, giving him a strong hug and a kiss.

"It's a promise. I love you."

"I'll count on hearing that every half hour."

Jordan squeezed her hand and gave her another swift kiss before meeting Braxton at the top of the stairs where he was waiting. They took one of the squad cars; in their experience, people were more likely to open up to people who were clearly police officers.

The first place they went was Kaitlin's school, Centennial High. They went inside and showed their badges in the front office.

"Hello, Mark," said the secretary brightly. The school serviced students in first grade through twelfth grade, and the same woman had been working in the front office for fifteen years. She had seen Jordan in here many times when

Kaitlin was younger, picking her up for appointments or trying to comfort her when she was having the separation anxieties that plague many young school children.

"Hi, Kathleen," Jordan replied. "Did you see my daughter leave school this afternoon?"

"Yes. And she left on time, too; she didn't skip any classes if that's what you're worried about."

"No, that's not what we're worried about, ma'am," said Braxton, in his gruff yet polite manner. "Can you tell us if she was with anybody when she left?"

"She was with Willow...Willow something. I can't remember her last name."

"Willow Jacobs," said Detective Jordan without missing a beat. "Those two girls are practically joined at the hip. I can't count how many times Willow Jacobs has been at my house eating dinner or having a sleepover with Kaitlin."

"Was Willow in drama club?" Braxton asked.

"Yes," said Jordan, following his partner's line of reasoning. "That means they were probably headed there together. Thank you for your help, Kathleen."

"Of course," Kathleen replied. She hesitated for a moment and then asked, "Is everything all right?"

"Fine," Detective Jordan lied. He hoped his face was convincing enough. Even if it wasn't, Kathleen decided to drop the matter.

"Have a nice evening, then," she said.

"And you as well," Braxton responded as he and Jordan left.

"Where to next?" Braxton asked as they got to the car. "The place where Kaitlin went to drama practice?"

"I think that would be best," said Jordan. "But let's not drive. If it's close enough for her to walk, then it's close enough for us, too. Besides, if we walk we're more likely to notice anything unusual."

Braxton agreed. As it was a very pleasant spring evening, they took their time, keeping their eyes on the ground in front of them for most of the time that they walked. Their destination was only about four blocks from the school. But Jordan and Braxton had only walked half of that distance when Jordan stopped dead, looking down an alleyway.

"Do you see something?" Braxton asked, noting the tension in his partner's body language.

"No. But I remember Kaitlin saying one time that she would sometimes use this alleyway to cut off some of the distance between school and drama club. It sparked a pretty big argument between us; I recognized the dangers of going down a dark alleyway and she apparently did not."

"So what was the outcome of the argument?" Braxton asked. "Did she get mad enough that she might walk down it anyway just to defy you?"

"No, I don't think she would do that," said Jordan, shaking his head slowly. "But she might use it if she were late leaving school and thought there was a chance that she would be late for practice. Apparently this director of theirs was very strict about punctuality. And if she was with Willow, then she probably thought it would be perfectly safe."

"I really don't want to ask this question, but I'm going to anyway because I need to: does Willow Jacobs have blond hair?"

"No. Her hair is red. She's an—"

And he stopped in midsentence. He stood there slack-jawed in the middle of the alley, his face very pale and his eyes very wide. In fact, he looked so much like he might be getting ready to faint that Braxton actually took a step forward and grabbed his arm.

"Mark? What's wrong, what is it? Are you okay?"

"I'm fine. I've just had another revelation. We need to get to the Jacobs' house right now."

"Care to explain yourself first so I don't look like a complete moron when we get there? I can't back your play without knowing what it is."

Jordan was already walking quickly back to the school where their car was parked, barely listening to what his partner was saying.

"I don't think my daughter wasn't the only one who was kidnapped today. Listen, don't talk to me until we get back to the school, all right? I need to get some things straight in my head."

Braxton nodded. They backed out of the school's tiny parking lot and Jordan started giving out directions. In between telling Braxton where to turn, he spoke about the epiphany he had had in the mouth of the alleyway.

"What I was going to say when I stopped in midsentence back there," Jordan began, "is that Willow Jacobs is Irish. I mean, full-blooded Irish."

"So you think Jon grabbed both of them?"

"Yes. Turn right at this light up here."

Braxton did so, and then said, "Wouldn't that mess up his schedule? His plan with the circle?"

"Actually I think Willow is the centerpiece of the whole thing. In one of the books that I was reading this afternoon it said that whatever sacrifice the Druids offered had to be a perfect victim. That would make the chances of crossing over into the other realm better. Oh, turn left. Sorry."

Braxton slammed on his brakes; Jordan had almost waited too late to give the instructions.

"So he's going to kill Willow and not himself?"

"No, he's going to somehow kill Willow and himself at the same time. So the window between the worlds will open and allow both of them through."

"I wonder who or what he's so eager to find on the other side? Maybe the captain knows if he's lost someone recently. Someone close to him."

"We can worry about that later. We're here now. Their house is that one on the right with the green van parked in front."

Chapter 16

JORDAN AND BRAXTON walked up to the front door and Braxton rang the bell. Jordan was busy ruminating on what he would say, how best to tell Willow's parents that their daughter might be dead soon. Delivering that sort of news was never easy, but it was so much harder when you actually knew the people you were delivering it to. Jordan sincerely hoped that he would never be put in this sort of situation again. Once was one time too many.

But he didn't have much time to dwell on that because Mr. Jacobs was already opening the door. That always seemed to be the way things happened; when you didn't want to talk to someone they actually responded and when you did want to talk to them you were met with nothing but silence.

"Oh hello, Mark," he said. Then he looked around as if he were slightly confused. "Willow said you wouldn't be taking her home until closer to ten tonight; that director is really working those kids hard. Too hard in my opinion."

Now it was Jordan and Braxton's turn to look confused. They exchanged glances with one another.

"David, this is my partner, Steven Braxton. Do you mind if we come inside for a moment?"

A faint look of worry came over David Jacobs' face. Jordan knew that look all too well; he had seen it in the eyes of every parent he had ever had to visit at home. David knew something bad was coming. It was probably even more of a giveaway that Jordan had not come alone, but with Detective Braxton. But he still remained courteous.

"Of course you can come inside. Our house is yours."

"Good evening, Mark," said Sarah, David's wife, as she came out from the kitchen. "And hello to you, sir," she added to Detective Braxton, whom she had never met before. "We've just finished our supper but there's some still left on the stove. May I offer it to you?"

Jordan's stomach growled when she said this; he had forgotten it until now, but he hadn't had a decent meal in quite a while.

"Thank you, Mrs. Jacobs," he said. "But I'm afraid my partner and I don't have time for that right now. We'd like to speak with you and your husband if you don't mind."

"Well, those dishes aren't going anywhere—although I wish they would. Let's go into the living room shall we?" She spoke cheerfully enough, but her eyes gave her away; they mirrored her husband's worry.

And then they were all seated on the various sofas and chairs in the room and Jordan had no more time to think about what to say. What was more, he knew that Braxton would not be likely to deliver the news himself; he believed (and rightly so) that Jordan had the better amount of tact when it came to these situations. Most of the time, Jordan was pleased to possess this gift, but not always. Not in times like these.

Mr. and Mrs. Jacobs were looking at him expectantly so Jordan opened his mouth and began to speak.

"What you said before, David, about Willow contacting you? When was that, exactly?"

"Oh, it was a few hours ago. The girls—that is to say Willow and your daughter—had just gotten to their drama practice and the director told them it was going to run late because they had a lot of work to do to get ready; hard to believe their opening night is next week." A frown appeared on Mr. Jacobs's face and he continued, "I was under the impression that you had stopped by the practice and offered to give Willow a ride home when you came to pick up Kaitlin. Apparently I was wrong. You don't think they planned on ditching their practice and going out to party, do you? I think one of the universities nearby is having some sort of spring fling tonight."

"Unfortunately, sir," said Braxton, "We think it might be a little more serious than that."

"Has something happened to her?" Sarah asked. Her voice was just a tiny squeak; it was clear that she was desperately trying to fight back tears. "Has something happened to my Willow?"

She reached for her husband's hand without looking down; she kept her eyes locked on Detective Jordan's face.

"We believe that Willow and Kaitlin may have been kidnapped by the Knifer," said Jordan.

At this, Mrs. Jacobs could not keep from crying any longer. She hid her face in her husband's shirt as he wrapped a strong arm around her shoulders. Now he was the one staring at Detective Jordan. He did not cry, although his green eyes appeared unnaturally bright.

"Explain yourself, please, Mark. What makes you jump to that conclusion?"

"I called Lisa and asked if she could pick Kaitlin up from drama practice," said Jordan, leaving out the specific details. "Normally Kaitlin just walks, but with the current state of things I was uncomfortable with that. Anyway, Lisa said she wouldn't mind that at all. She got to the practice space a bit early, and discovered that there was nobody there. Apparently the director had come down with the flu and cancelled rehearsal for the day."

"And because it was light, the girls probably thought they would be safe if they walked, as long as they were together," Braxton added.

"But you still haven't explained," Mr. Jacobs insisted. "What proof do you have that this serial killer is responsible?"

And what could Jordan say? Certainly he couldn't tell them the truth: that the police had let the killer enter into the investigation, given him full access to all the information they had. Handed him weapons to use against them.

"I can't tell you what proof I have due to the limitations of the law," Jordan said. Even as he spoke, he resented himself; he despised hiding behind the law, and he thought it would be a great relief to just say what he was actually thinking and get it all off his chest. "But I can tell you that the evidence we've collected shows that your daughter will probably be the Knifer's last victim. What's more, we have some idea of when that event will take place, and we still have time to stop him. But we need your help to do that."

"Of course," said David, after a moment or two in which the only sound to be heard was his wife struggling to keep her tears in check. "Whatever you need to help you get her back to us safe and sound."

"Thank you," Jordan sighed in relief.

"First of all," Braxton said, taking over from his partner, "we'll need some more information about the call you got from Willow. Do you know an exact time that you got the message?"

"I can do better than that," said David, getting up from the couch after disentangling himself gently from his wife's death grip. "She called the house phone and I haven't deleted the voicemail yet."

He pressed a few buttons and then the answering machine's usual spiel came on, informing everyone in the room that there were no new messages and one saved message. David Jacobs pressed the button required to play the saved messages and the machine rattled off the date, time, and approximate length of the call. Braxton dutifully scribbled down all of this information in his little notebook. Then Willow's voice filled the room.

"Hey, it's me," she said. "Listen, practice is going to run late tonight. But Kaitlin talked to her dad and he said he would give us a ride home. So...I guess I'll see you later. Like around nine or ten or so. I love you. Bye."

"Do you need me to replay it?" David Jacobs asked over the renewed smooth flow of the answering machine lady's robotic voice.

Jordan shook his head but his partner said, "Yes. Play it again."

Jordan looked at him questioningly. "Did you hear something I didn't?"

"I won't know unless you let me listen very closely."

Jordan took the hint and shut his mouth. Braxton didn't seem to pay the first part of the message any undue attention, but he leaned forward during the second half of it.

"So...I guess I'll see you later. Like around nine or ten or so. I love you. Bye."

"Did you hear it?" Braxton asked.

"Hear what?" Jordan said, frustrated that he wasn't getting it—which of course only further lessened his ability to pick up on whatever it was that his partner was hearing. "I only heard that the message was very short—probably too short to do us any good."

"That remains to be seen, but we'll worry about that later," said Braxton, waving away what Jordan saw as important as though it were not important at all. "Mr. Jacobs, one more time please."

Mr. Jacobs did as he was bidden.

"Those pauses that she makes before 'so' and 'I love you': it makes it sound like she was under duress when she made that phone call."

"So she was already with the Knifer at that time."

"Exactly," Braxton replied. "But more importantly, she *and Kaitlin* were with the Knifer."

"Wait a minute…when she said the word 'dad' she put a special emphasis on it. Like she was trying to draw attention to that particular word without being overly obvious about it."

"I don't understand," said Mrs. Jacobs. "What does that mean? Why would she be putting an emphasis on that word?"

"What it means, Mrs. Jacobs, is that your daughter is brilliant. Could you excuse my partner and I for just a moment, please?"

Without waiting for a reply, he made his way through the kitchen and out of the sliding glass door onto the back deck. How many times had he stood on these same wooden boards grilling or eating hamburgers and talking about the latest football game? Now he was standing here trying to decipher a thirty second message.

"Kaitlin and Willow knew they were in trouble so they were trying to leave us a hint," said Braxton. "You raised her up well, Mark."

Jordan smiled a little at that, the first time he'd smiled all afternoon.

"Now we just have to be clever enough to figure out what that message was," he said.

There was silence for a few moments while both of them stared in opposite directions, trying to puzzle it out. It was Braxton who got there first.

"Why would she specify the time?"

"Nine or ten… the time she's going to die?"

Jordan looked at his watch and panicked a little as he said this; if Willow was going to die at around nine or ten o'clock, then their deadline was even tighter than they had previously imagined.

"No," said Braxton, with a certainty that made Jordan look up at him in surprise. "Willow is going to be killed last, remember? And that means Kaitlin has to die first." He seemed to replay what he had just said in his head because his eyes suddenly grew very wide. "Not that that's going to happen. Kaitlin isn't going to die either. Of course she won't, I won't let that happen and I know you won't either."

"Look, Steve, I'm only going to say this once, so pay attention all right?" When Braxton had nodded, Jordan continued, "Stop walking on eggshells around me, like you're afraid I'll snap if I hear my daughter's name. It wastes time, and it puts me more on edge. Got it?"

"Got it," said Braxton meekly.

"Good. So to summarize, we have just under two hours to save Willow and my daughter, and we have no idea where Jon is going to kill them," said Jordan, resigning himself to what seemed like the impossible.

"No," Braxton. "I told you already, the time that she mentioned isn't the time he's going to kill them."

"But it's supposed to be a full moon tonight; he would have to kill them tonight to get the right shadow, so we still only have until midnight, or at the very latest, until the sun starts coming up tomorrow."

"But she wasn't talking about time at all!" Braxton exclaimed.

Jordan stared at him in disbelief, trying to wrap his head around it. But he found that he couldn't.

"What are you getting at?" Jordan asked. "It sure sounded like the time to me."

"Exactly, and that just speaks to Willow's brilliance," Braxton replied. "But what if it was actually a location?"

"Ninth and Tenth Avenues in New York City!" Jordan exclaimed.

"We need to call Longhorn," said Braxton. "He and Detective Lynch are much closer than we are."

"And then we need to head up there to back them up," said Jordan. He no longer wanted to be there so that he could say he was involved in catching a serial killer and bringing him to justice. Now he just wanted to be there to hold his daughter and give her a big, comforting hug as he rescued her.

"Agreed. I'll call Longhorn and the captain, you tell the Jacobs family what's going on. But remember, no specifics."

"Right," said Jordan. And he dashed back into the house, leaving his partner outside to make the necessary phone calls.

Chapter 17

"WE HAVE SOME good news, Mr. and Mrs. Jacobs," Jordan said as he walked in. "We think we know where your daughter is being held, and we have detectives on their way there right now. My partner and I are going to head up there ourselves just as soon as we finish up here. We're going to find her."

"I believe you," said Mr. Jacobs. "And you're going to find your own daughter, too. All this time you've been here we've been focusing on our baby girl when yours is in danger too. That's rather selfish of us, isn't it?"

"How do you think I could blame you for caring about your daughter?" Detective Jordan asked. "But rest assured, I'll bring her home to you."

"Her life is in your hands," said Mrs. Jacobs. "Please be careful. May the road rise up to meet you. And may the wind be ever at your back."

"That's the Old Irish way of saying good luck and stay safe," David explained, managing a small smile.

Jordan smiled too, but in reality the phrase had the exact opposite effect of cheering him. It came from "The Irish Blessing," a song he most closely associated with funerals. But he shook off that feeling; there would be no funerals, not tonight. Not for the girls, and not for any of the detectives involved in the case.

Before Jordan had a chance to say anything else, Braxton entered the room with his cell phone open in his hand and his fingers covering the mouthpiece.

"Captain wants a word with both of us," he said quietly.

"Go," said Mr. Jacobs. "And please keep us updated."

"That's a promise," said Jordan, opening the front door to follow Braxton out to the car.

"Mark," David Jacobs said, and Jordan turned back. "One way or the other. Understood?"

He seemed to be resigning himself to the fact that the update he received might not be good news. Jordan desperately wanted to tell him that the news would be good, no matter what. But he had already made several promises tonight that he wasn't sure he would be able to keep.

So he just said, "Understood," and walked outside. Braxton handed his phone to Jordan and got behind the wheel. A few moments later they were speeding on their way to New York. As they drove, Captain Huntington continued the conversation that he and Braxton had already begun.

"Steve, have you already called Longhorn and Lynch to update them, tell them where to go?"

"Yes," Braxton answered. "And Charles said that he's going to call in a few favors with some of the guys up there that he works with; he wants to find out what sort of buildings are on Ninth and Tenth Avenue so there are no unpleasant surprises."

"I don't blame him for that. I've phoned the forensics team and told them to trace both Willow's cell phone and Kaitlin's. Right now there's no signal, but they said they'll let us know if there's any change in that."

"Jon's smart; he's probably had the phones destroyed by this point, or else he's taken the battery out," said Braxton.

Normally Jordan disapproved of his partner's pessimistic nature, but he thought Braxton was probably right in this case. The silence from the other end of the line indicated that Huntington agreed with Braxton's assessment as well.

"Would they be able to possibly tell us where Willow's cell phone was when she phoned her parents?" Jordan asked. "That would at least give us some kind of idea about where they were headed, and if the timeline matches up with them being taken to Ninth and Tenth Avenues."

"They're trying, but it's going to take some time. And they wouldn't be able to give an exact location, just an estimate based on what tower the cell phone signal bounced off of to make the call."

"How not exact is not exact?" Braxton asked.

"The technician I spoke to said that based on the length of the call, they could give us an estimate of about ten miles in any one direction. So pretty much the only help that's going to give you is, like Mark said, to tell you if you were right in guessing where they were headed."

"Is there any other information we need that we're missing?" Braxton asked. "Anything that might help us out?"

"Not right now. But as soon as I know anything more, I'll pass it on to you."

"All right then. So long for now, Captain."

"Be careful, the both of you."

Jordan ended the call but immediately started dialing another number.

"What are you doing?" his partner asked him.

"I'm calling our friend Detective Longhorn. I have a theory that I want to run by him, and by you. I might as well say it just once."

But Longhorn didn't answer his phone. Jordan left a message, but he kept it short, and also very unrevealing. He was learning from Jon Hall.

"Try Lynch's phone," Braxton suggested, while Jordan's fingers were already moving on the keypad.

Detective Lynch didn't answer either, so Jordan left another message. He waited five minutes and then tried each number again, with the exact same results.

"What is going on?" he muttered.

"You know, usually assuming the worst is my job."

"Well, this isn't your typical case."

"No. I suppose it's not." Something in Braxton's tone made Jordan look over from the passenger seat and inspect his partner's face. It didn't take him long to figure out what Braxton was trying to imply with that statement.

"You think the captain was wrong to let me keep working this case."

"No, of course not," Braxton said, but he made a point of keeping his eyes on the road, instead of looking his partner in the face. Jordan gave a little disbelieving laugh and looked out of the passenger's window.

"You're lying," he said simply. "You don't think I can handle this. Nobody thinks I can."

"Do you think you can?" Braxton asked.

"Of course I do. I wouldn't be here if I thought I couldn't."

"Okay. Then that's all that matters. As long as you have trust and confidence in your own abilities that's all you need."

"That's not all I need," Jordan contradicted him. "I need my partner to trust that I can take care of myself, and that I'll also look after him."

"Mark, I put my life in your hands every day that we work together. I think that's pretty much the definition of trust. And I hope you know that I have your back, too, and that means more than just protecting you if something goes wrong while we're on the job. It seems to me like you're scared that showing any kind of emotion in regards to this case is going to jeopardize your chances of solving it. But the same thing is true if you keep everything bottled up inside. You can talk to me if you need to; I just wanted to be sure you knew that."

This was normally an unspoken agreement between the two of them, and Jordan had never really found the need to take advantage of it. But to hear Braxton say it out loud meant a lot to Jordan at that moment, and did a great deal to calm his nerves.

As he was trying to find some appropriate way to respond, the phone in his lap started to vibrate. Jordan looked at the caller ID and flipped it on speaker.

"Charles, where are you right now? I tried calling twice."

"I know, sorry I missed you. We're at Jon Hall's office; it was right on the way and we figured we would at least check it out in case he was holding the girls here. Who knows, maybe the address we got was just the kill site. Anyway, they aren't here, and neither is he. But there are signs that he's been here recently, or someone has."

"What kind of signs?" Braxton asked.

"Why are you still there instead of searching for my daughter and her friend?" Jordan demanded at the same time.

"Mark's question first: we're leaving now, we just had to keep the crime scene secure until the forensics crew from New York arrived. It's in their hands now. And moving on to Steve's question: the office was rather disorderly, and suspiciously so."

"That's all you've got?" Braxton said scathingly. "Have you ever even been to his office? The one time we went it was a complete pig sty."

"Yes, but with Jon everything is organized chaos. But that wasn't the case this time. This time it looked like he had been searching for something very important that he needed to find very quickly. This might have taken place, for example, around 4:45, when he found out we were on to him."

"So Kaitlin and Willow might have been there at some point," Jordan deduced. "The psycho could have had them in the room while he was talking to us."

That was a truly haunting thought to him, that his daughter could have been hearing his voice, feeling desperate for help and yet powerless to communicate with him.

"It's a possibility," Longhorn agreed. "But the point we need to focus on is that he's not there now. I have a friend who works in the surveillance unit of the FBI who owes me a favor. He's currently looking at everything from red light cameras to ATM cams trying to find Jonathan and possibly the girls. They're checking back footage as well, trying to track Jon's route once he left his office."

"I envy your connections," said Braxton.

"Well, what can I say?" Longhorn replied, and both Jordan and Braxton could hear the smile in his voice. "I'm a likeable sort of guy."

"Getting back to the actual point," Jordan said, "Charles, do you remember any of the other victims' parents mentioning getting a call from their children the day they were killed? Or at least the day that they were reported missing?"

"Yes actually. But only the last two victims. That is, the ones from Connecticut. I wonder why that is?"

"This is Jon we're talking about," said Detective Jordan. "I bet he's been taking a recording so it can trigger a memory for him—so he can remember how scared they sounded as they talked to their parents for the last time. I guess for the victims in New York he could just go visit the crime scenes to trigger the memories. Or look at the pictures that got leaked to the newspapers."

"That seems like a plausible explanation," Longhorn said.

"Let's hope our friend Jonathan was less careful about leaving evidence in his office than at his crime scenes," said Braxton.

"I'm sure he was less careful," Jordan said. "It would have aroused suspicion if someone had come in and he was wearing gloves and spraying down any hard surfaces with bleach or Lysol."

"True enough," Longhorn agreed. After a pause he added, "Detective Lynch and I are about forty-five minutes away from Ninth and Tenth. Some other detectives from my squad are headed there now as well. They'll get there before we do but we've told them to just unobtrusively observe. We don't want to spook him."

"You said you've worked with him before during previous investigations," Braxton pointed out. "Isn't there a possibility that he might recognize one of your detective's faces?"

"We were careful to involve only those squad members whom Jon has never seen or heard. They should get there soon. Actually, hang on…" His voice became muffled and then came back again stronger. "I'm getting another call coming in right now, it might be them. I'll get back to you in a few minutes."

Longhorn and Jordan hung up their respective phones and there was silence once more. Jordan knew it would not do him any good to just sit and dwell on whatever was happening in New York, but he couldn't help doing exactly that. He felt so powerless; whatever his daughter was going through, he couldn't comfort her for at least another hour. That's how long it would take him and Braxton to get to the heart of New York City where they needed to be.

Jordan's cell phone rang again and he glanced at the caller ID, his hand already on the accept button. He expected it to be either Detective Lynch or Detective Longhorn. But now his finger hesitated. The call was coming from Kaitlin's cell phone.

"Hey," Braxton said, who had also seen who was calling. "Speaker phone. I'll keep my mouth shut."

Jordan nodded, took a deep breath, and pressed accept and then the speaker button.

"Hello?" he said.

"Daddy?" came the reply. Just that one word broke his heart; Kaitlin never called him that unless she was very, very scared.

"Hi, Kaitlin."

For his daughter's sake he tried to keep his voice as calm as possible. He couldn't directly assure her because Jonathan was probably listening to this call right now, but he also wanted to keep her talking; that would give their own computer team time to trace the call and get them an exact location. To Kaitlin's credit, she managed to hold back her tears even though he knew she must be terrified.

"Willow and I went out to catch a movie and get some dinner because drama practice ended early. She called her parents and lied to say that the practice ran late; they're always so strict on her and never let her go anywhere except if it's school-related."

"How soon will you be home?" Jordan asked. And then he took a risk. "Do you want me to come pick you guys up?"

"No, no we'll be fine. We should be home at around nine or ten o'clock. I just wanted to let you know so you wouldn't worry like you always do. And especially lately with the Knifer running around and stuff."

Kaitlin was taking risks of her own then, especially with that last statement. At first, Jordan's initial reaction was to be proud of his daughter's courage; she was in fact very much like him, maybe more so than either of them realized. But then his reason caught up with his emotions. Why should he be proud of her for taking such huge risks when her life was at stake?

"Okay, sweetheart. As long as you're sure."

"I'm sure." But her voice was quiet, and quivering just a little, like she wouldn't be able to hold back the tears much longer.

And Jordan knew it was time to get off the phone, more for her sake than for his own. He knew that she would be punished if she started to cry, thereby alerting her father to the fact that something was wrong. So he did the best thing he could do in that situation, even though it went against every paternal instinct he had: he pretended not to notice that his daughter was upset.

"All right then, sweetie. Just stay safe and I'll see you soon, okay?"

"Okay, Dad. Love you."

"Love you too. So long, kiddo."

"Bye," Kaitlin whispered. And then she was gone.

Chapter 18

ALMOST BEFORE JORDAN hung up, Braxton's phone started going off. Jordan thought if he ever heard another phone ringing it would be too soon. It was their captain who was calling, informing them that the forensics technician had just succeeded in tracing a call from Kaitlin's cell phone.

"They can't tell where the call went, and I guess they can't know if it was really her on the phone or just somebody else using it. But either way, they got a general location, and it looks like we were right: the girls—or at least their cell phones—are somewhere along Ninth Avenue, between Ninth and Tenth."

"I know the answers to both of the questions that the forensics technicians can't answer," said Jordan. "The call was placed to me and it really was Kaitlin on the phone."

"So she's alive?"

"Yes. And she was giving me all sorts of hints just like I was giving her hints. I only hope that she was able to pick up on them and he wasn't."

"What kind of hints?"

"She said she and Willow got out of drama early so they went out together. She said Willow lied to her parents. That was my first clue; she emphasized the words *drama* and *lied*. And her voice even sounded like she was reading a script or something at that point. It was subtle but it was definitely there."

"Okay. What else?"

"She said she thought they would be home about nine or ten o'clock. That's the same thing Willow said to her parents."

"So that, along with the call trace, confirms the location. That's good. You have a smart kid, Mark."

"She takes after her father," Braxton chimed in. Jordan rolled his eyes, but also flashed his partner a grateful smile.

"That much is clear," Huntington replied. "Now what about the hints you were giving her?"

"When she said she was going to be out late, I asked her if she wanted me to come pick her up. I know it was a risk, but I feel like it's what every sensible and responsible parent would say in that situation. And she said 'No', but she said it twice. It's a trick I taught her a few years ago, when she had just turned thirteen. I told her that I wouldn't be the stereotypical overprotective father; I would let her go out with her friends, and be a normal teenager but there were some safety measures that we should agree on first. One of the things I told her about was that if she was ever in a situation that made her uncomfortable, but she didn't want to or couldn't say that out loud, she should say 'No' twice when I asked her a yes or no question. That way I would know that she was in trouble and needed someone to come get her."

"I bet you never thought she would have to use that little trick," said Huntington.

"No, I didn't. But it's a good thing I taught it to her."

"Yes, it certainly is. Were there any other clues flying between the two of you?"

"She said the reason she called was because she knew I would be worried, what with the Knifer running around."

The captain's response was to give a low whistle. Jordan couldn't tell if this was to indicate that he was impressed with Kaitlin's nerve or that he was worried for her with the risk she had taken. Possibly it was a mixture of both.

"After that, she almost started crying, so I knew it was time to get off the phone. But before I did, I took a risk of my own. I told her I would see her soon. I figure if Jon was listening, he would just think I'd be expecting to see her after she got home."

But even as Jordan said that, it sounded like a bit of a weak reason for taking what really was a huge risk. Sure enough, the captain's reply made it clear that he was more than a little unhappy with his detective.

"I told you I would let you stay on this case and I'm going to keep that promise. Not much I can do about it right now anyways, given the fact that you're halfway to another state. But you're skating on very thin ice here, Mark. Jon already knows that we're on to him, and now he knows we're on our way. You do realize that you may have just put your daughter and Willow Jacobs in even greater danger?"

Before Captain Huntington could really wind up and get going, Jordan interrupted him.

"I want to speak to my wife, Captain. I want to let her know that her daughter is alive, at least for the time being. I want to give her at least a little bit of comfort, and I can only hope that she didn't hear what you said to me just now; otherwise giving her that comfort is going to be a lot harder."

"She didn't overhear," the captain said, sighing. "And I'm sorry if I spoke harshly, but I still disagree with the decision you made. I think that's something you need to keep in mind. I'll go and get your wife now. Hold on a second."

So Jordan listened to the muffled background noises of the police station. A few minutes later, he heard Lisa's voice.

"Mark? Is everything all right? The captain said there was news."

"I got a call from Kaitlin. She's alive. And she's where we thought she was."

"Was Kaitlin okay? Does she know you're coming?"

"She sounded...scared. But not as though she were in pain, not as though he had hurt her. And she didn't sound scared enough that it made me think these might be her last few minutes alive."

At these words there was a muffled little cry.

"I'm sorry," Jordan said immediately. "I shouldn't have phrased it that way. But to answer your next question: I couldn't tell her outright that I was coming to get her—that would be too dangerous given the fact that the killer was probably listening in on the conversation. But I hinted at it, and Kaitlin's probably clever enough to have picked up on it. She was feeding me a lot of subtle clues as well. That's a good sign; it means that even though she's scared, she's able to think through that fear and keep her wits about her."

"She is clever," Jordan's wife said. "You did a good job bringing her up."

"I couldn't have done it without you," said Jordan, allowing himself another smile. His wife had the incredible ability to see the best even in a terrible situation and to make others see it, too.

"You be sure to tell her how much we love her."

"I will. We're getting closer to her, so I can't talk much longer."

"I understand. Go. Do your job. And get our daughter back."

Jordan ended the call and then leaned back in his seat. Braxton gave him what he wanted most: silence, and time to collect his thoughts and gear up for the night ahead.

After a little while, Jordan checked his watch.

"You must be speeding. We shouldn't be this close behind Longhorn and Lynch."

"If you have a problem with my driving, you can always arrest me," Braxton joked.

"Actually I was going to ask if you wanted to put the siren on so we could go even faster."

Braxton did so, and people accordingly moved out of their way.

"We should probably turn it off as we get closer, though," said Braxton as he went through a red light. "Don't want Jonathan to get spooked."

"Actually I think I disagree with you."

"What makes you say that?"

"Because Longhorn and Lynch and whatever backup Longhorn has arranged for are probably going to be thinking the same way that you are. But there are always sirens going off in New York, so silence might actually be more suspicious than noise."

"I see your point. But we're not there yet, so for now let's just get psyched up to do this."

Jordan pulled out his phone to turn it on vibrate so it wouldn't give away their position. But it rang before he could.

"Longhorn again. They must be there already. What is it, Charles?"

"It's Lynch actually. Longhorn's talking to some of the guys on his squad."

"You guys are at Ninth and Tenth, then?" Braxton asked.

"Yeah. And we found an old building that looks like the perfect place to hide two girls that have been recently kidnapped. There's some construction going on at the place next door, too, so the noise would hide any screams or cries for help."

"Sounds promising," said Braxton. Then he glanced at his partner and amended himself. "Well, it's not promising that their screams won't be heard. What I meant was that it sounds like a probable location. Sorry Mark," he muttered as an afterthought.

In response, Jordan leaned into the mouthpiece of the phone and spoke very clearly.

"As I've already told my partner, everyone needs to stop acting so awkward around me. Not only is it obnoxious, but it's making it that much harder for me to be objective here. And for Pete's sake, please stop worrying about me getting my feelings hurt by something you say. I'm a big boy, I know how to suck it up and deal with it. Do I make myself clear?"

"Yes," Detective Lynch answered after a moment or two. "You are very much understood, sir. I'll make sure Detective Longhorn gets the message as well."

"And don't forget Longhorn's backup from his squad in New York," Detective Jordan added.

"You won't need to worry about them. They only know the first names of the victims. Longhorn made sure of that."

"Thank you," Jordan said in a far calmer tone. "Now, what are you doing about this promising location you mentioned?"

"Some of Longhorn's guys are checking it out. But quietly, so as not to attract attention. Oh, and he got another one of his buddies from the FBI to scan it with some heat-sensing satellite or some such high-tech, fancy piece of equipment. We're trying to get as much information as we possibly can so we don't go storming in there blind."

"Just how many buddies does Longhorn have in the FBI?" Braxton asked. "He didn't used to work for them did he?"

"I don't know," Lynch said, and Jordan thought he could hear him grinning. For some reason it was hard to picture Longhorn as a federal agent without feeling the urge to laugh hysterically. "But right now I'm just glad there are some people out there who are willing to help us out. We were going to wait for the two of you to get here so we can cover as much ground as we can in the least amount of time possible."

His tone of voice told Jordan that there was another unspoken reason: Longhorn and Lynch both knew how much Jordan wanted to be there when whatever was going to happen actually went down. Jordan appreciated that sentiment but he had to ask himself if waiting was putting his daughter in more danger than she was already in. Then again, how much would not waiting add to the danger level for the officers and detectives that were already there?

"How far out are we?" Jordan asked his partner.

"About ten minutes or so," Braxton answered.

"How long is it going to take Longhorn's mysterious buddy to finish scanning the building?" Jordan asked now of Detective Lynch. He heard Lynch shout the question over his shoulder and listen to the reply before coming back on the line.

"About ten minutes."

"That works out perfectly then. We'll see you soon."

"We'll be here," Lynch answered, and then hung up.

Chapter 19

WHEN JORDAN AND Braxton finally arrived, they found a cluster of six men gathered around the hood of a police cruiser. Braxton parked next to them, but not too close, and he parked facing the opposite direction. That way they would be able to block Jonathan off from both directions if he decided to make a run for it.

After a general round of introductions—much of which Jordan paid no attention to—and an obligatory round of handshaking, the real work began: analyzing all the data that Longhorn's FBI contacts had collected. The satellite that Lynch had mentioned had picked up three weak heat signals coming from the building.

"Weak?" Jordan asked. "Weak like the signatures were cold?"

He couldn't bring himself to say the word "dead."

"Weak as in they were farther away from the satellite," one of Longhorn's detectives explained. "In other words, they're probably in the basement or on the first floor somewhere."

"Basement makes more sense in my opinion," Braxton said, and there was a general murmur of assent throughout the group. Now another one of Longhorn's detectives—a man named Reggie Thyme, who looked like he wouldn't be out of place on a football field—spoke up.

"The six of us are also in agreement that the best course of action would be to send three men in first to clear the first floor. No kicking in the door, either; the less noise we make the better. Once the first floor checks out, the rest of you will get a signal that it's safe to come inside, and we'll all go down to the basement together."

"Sounds like a solid plan," said Jordan, studying the layout of the first floor. There was a door just off the lobby that concealed the staircase down to the basement. "I'll take the lead after the first floor is cleared."

"You're that eager to put your life on the line?" asked Reggie. His voice wasn't antagonistic exactly, but he did sound suspicious.

"Actually, letting him go first might save all our lives," said Braxton before Jordan had a chance to say anything.

"Some partner you are," Detective Matthews scoffed.

"I'm not saying he can go first because I have some 'better him than me' mentality," Braxton fired back at once. "I'm saying he should go first because he's absolutely incredible at talking people down. I've seen it a hundred times since I started working with him, and it never fails to amaze me."

"I've seen it, too," Detective Lynch spoke up. "It's a completely unique gift. And if we could get the kidnapper to come with us willingly, with no shots fired, I think it would be better for everybody involved."

Reggie Thyme looked directly at Detective Jordan and asked, "If you can't talk him down, will you still be able to act? In other words, will you shoot if necessary?"

"That man killed six innocent young women, and we have evidence that he's planning two more murders. The only way he's leaving that building is in handcuffs or a body bag."

Reggie and the other detectives from New York all gave Jordan appraising looks, trying to figure out what to think about this man who could talk down and diffuse a situation, and yet spoke so violently.

"Good to know," Reggie said finally. "Me, Raymond, and Longhorn will clear the first floor. Once we give the all clear, the three of you from Connecticut will come in and we can go down to the basement."

"What about them?" Braxton asked. He had forgotten the names of the other two detectives from Longhorn's squad but he didn't much care about that at the moment. He had more pressing concerns on his mind.

"They're the two newest members of the squad," Longhorn explained. "Their job is to take care of the perimeter in case Jon decides to make a run for it. Which would be a stupid idea when he's faced with six cops, but all the same."

Longhorn shrugged and let the sentence hang. His tone gave Jordan the impression that what he really wanted to say was that because the young men were so new, they couldn't be trusted in such an important operation. That was why they were being assigned to a job that, while still important, was out of the line of direct action.

"If everyone's ready, then let's get this show on the road," said Reggie, who seemed to be the most senior member there.

With that order everyone took their positions, and Reggie quietly edged open the front door. Jordan's heart began to beat a little harder as the darkness inside the building swallowed up the three men who entered. He couldn't help but think of all the things that could go wrong. But very soon—much sooner than Jordan had been expecting actually—Detective Raymond appeared at the front door again and silently waved the three of them in. The two rookies, their faces pale but determined, started patrolling the perimeter as Lynch, Jordan and Braxton entered the building.

Once they were inside, it was clear that the building had definitely not been in use for quite some time. Dust lay thickly on the floor of the sweeping lobby, and on the top of what appeared to be a receptionist's desk a few feet away to their right. But the dust would also help to lessen the sound of their footsteps, so that was a good thing. Looking closely, Jordan could see three sets of foot-prints leading toward the basement door. He drew his weapon and walked slowly toward the door that led to the basement, with Detective Lynch on his left and Detective Braxton on his right; both were slightly behind him. The three men from New York hung back a little, two of them facing backwards to cover the entrance of the building in case they had missed anything. Jordan placed his hand on the doorknob and then turned around with raised eyebrows, silently asking if everybody was ready.

When he had received five nods he opened the door, thanking his lucky stars that it didn't creak. The small amount of light that filtered through from the lobby allowed him to see a set of stairs but not much else. After listening for a moment and hearing nothing but silence, Jordan went through the door and started down. Five times, the light from the doorway was blocked out and Jordan knew that his backup was behind him. They went down two flights of stairs, and the farther down they went, the colder and darker it got.

There was another door when they reached the bottom of the stairs. It was just an ordinary door—nothing scary about it at all—and yet Jordan found that he was scared. *Jonathan could be waiting behind that door with a knife, ready to attack,* he thought, and the fear increased. But then he told himself, *My daughter could be behind that door.* And he knew he would be able to find the courage needed to do what he had to do—no matter what that might be.

He looked behind him one last time. "Ready?" he mouthed. Everyone indicated that they were, so Jordan held up three fingers on his left hand. His right hand held the gun steady. He slowly put down one finger, then the second and finally the third. Then he yanked the door open and banged inside. Noise wasn't the concern now, unless you counted being concerned about making as much noise as possible. Surprise was most definitely the greatest advantage they had, and nothing surprised somebody like a nice loud noise right near them.

But at first glance it looked like the room was empty other than a few old boilers in the far corner. Then Jordan caught movement out of the corner of his eye. He raised his gun in that direction, his finger tightening around the trigger; then somebody from behind him turned on a flashlight and shone it right into the face of the person hurtling toward Detective Jordan.

Chapter 20

Kaitlin threw her hand up to shield her eyes.

"It's me, it's me, please don't shoot me. He's not here. Daddy, please you have to go and find him, he took Willow. He said he's going to kill her."

Jordan moved out of the way of the doorway and the five men behind him swept in to clear the room. Once they made sure they were alone they all lowered their weapons and somebody turned on the light switch that was just inside the door. Kaitlin looked dirty and scared, and her cheek was red as though she had been slapped. But otherwise she looked none the worse for wear.

Jordan holstered his gun and Kaitlin jumped into his arms, the tears starting to run down her cheeks. He held her and whispered "I love you" over and over again into her ear until she calmed down.

"Let me get this straight," said Reggie angrily. "One of the victims is your daughter and your captain actually let you stay on this case?"

"Yes, this is my daughter," Jordan replied, matching Reggie's anger. "And I wanted to be first into the basement because I wanted my face to be the first one that she saw. I've already been given multiple lectures by my captain, so before you waste time giving me another one, I think we need to remember that Kaitlin wasn't the only girl kidnapped."

Reggie shook his head but let the matter drop. "Where did this guy go, Miss Jordan? We didn't see any footprints leading up the stairs."

"There's a door over there by that boiler. I guess it's a delivery hatch or something. He had his knife but he had a gun too. He kept it trained on me, and the knife at her throat. He said he would be coming back for me, and that he'd planted alarms and tracking devices and stuff all around this room and that he'd kill me if I tried to escape. I know now that he was probably lying but I was just so scared. And I didn't want him to hurt Willow."

"It's OK, Kaitlin," said Braxton. His voice was gentle, but his eyes were sharp and attentive. "When did this happen?"

"He left about an hour ago, right after he made me call you, Dad. I think it was my fault. I was trying to give you clues but I think I gave away too much."

"Listen to me, sweetheart," said Jordan, taking her face in both of his hands. "That was a brilliant phone call, and this wasn't your fault. If anything it was my fault, dropping those clues of my own even though I knew the risks. Now did he say anything about where he was going?"

"He just said he was taking her home. And that soon they would both be going to their real home. Daddy, what does that even mean?"

"I don't know for sure," Jordan hedged, although he thought it was a reference to the final murder-suicide that Jon was planning. "Longhorn, do you have his home address?"

"Right here," Longhorn said, pulling out his phone and staring at the information on the screen. "He was foolish enough to invite me over for dinner. Probably just trying to gain my trust, but I saved the information."

"That's just three blocks from here," said Detective Raymond, looking over Longhorn's shoulder.

"All right then. Let's move out," Reggie commanded.

"Not all of us," Longhorn said. "I'm going to escort Detective Jordan and his daughter back to our precinct."

"That's a good idea," Reggie agreed. "We'll meet you back there once we finish up at Jonathan's house. You can give the report to Captain Kay about what happened here tonight."

"Will do. Come on Mark, Kaitlin."

And they all filed upstairs. Jordan, Longhorn, and Kaitlin all clambered into Longhorn's car and they headed off toward the police station, which was apparently a ten-minute drive away. In the rearview mirror Jordan watched his partner get into a car with one of the other detectives—he couldn't quite tell who from this distance—and head off in the opposite direction. Part of Jordan felt that he should be watching his partner's back, but the other part of him—the paternal part, which was the strongest bit of him just now—knew that his duty was to his daughter.

He pulled out his phone and passed it to her in the backseat.

"I think your mother would like to hear from you," he told her.

Kaitlin grinned—it was a real smile this time, no doubt about that—and dialed her mother's cell phone number by heart. Even though Jordan could only hear half of the reunion that followed, it warmed his heart to know that no harm had come to his family tonight. After about five minutes of alternate laughing and crying, Kaitlin passed the phone back to her father.

"Captain Huntington said he wants a quick word with you," she said.

"Hello, Captain."

"One abductee safe, then," said Huntington. "Congratulations on that. But what about Willow and the Knifer himself?"

"The two of them apparently left about an hour ago," said Jordan. "We think they might be at Jonathan's residence; Braxton and some of Longhorn's men are headed over there right now and Longhorn is taking me and Kaitlin to the police station so that she can get some rest."

"Let me know as soon as you hear anything about Willow; her father has been regularly checking in with me for updates."

"Will do, Captain," Jordan said.

"And Mark," Huntington said before Jordan could hang up. "I really am glad your daughter is safe. I'm going to drive up there myself and escort your wife so she can see Kaitlin."

"I look forward to that," said Jordan, smiling. There was still a lot of pressure on him—after all, Jonathan was still on the loose—but he felt oddly detached from it all now. And he thought he had earned that momentary escape.

Chapter 21

THERE WAS A little lounge upstairs at the police station where Longhorn said Kaitlin could wait for her mother to arrive. He also pointed out a room with some cots in it in case she wanted to grab a nap. Then he left to go give his captain the report of what had happened and left Jordan and his daughter alone.

"I'm still too keyed up to sleep right now," Kaitlin said, yawning as she spoke. She leaned her head against her father's shoulder. Jordan let her sit quietly for a moment, enjoying the quiet himself. But then he cleared his throat.

"I don't want to ask you this, honey, but I have to. What happened this afternoon?"

Kaitlin turned maybe half a shade paler, but she answered his question anyway.

"Willow and I walked over to drama practice, but there was a note on the door from the director; he's sick, so practice was cancelled. We were just going to go over to Willow's house and hang out, enjoy the afternoon together. I was just about to call Mom and let her know where I'd be when this van pulled up beside us.

"Being your daughter, I got a little antsy right away, so I kept my distance from the doors and windows. The guy driving—the Knifer—had a New York accent, but only a little bit. He joked with us that half of his house was in Connecticut and half was in New York but he still managed to get lost in both states. He asked for directions to the highway and I gave them to him. He drove off in one direction, and Willow and I started walking the other way. But then I heard a car accelerating behind us, and a door slammed. Before either of us could turn around, somebody else jumped out of the back of the van and dragged us in by our backpacks."

"So he wasn't acting alone?" Jordan asked, breaking in for the first time. "Did you hear him address this other man?"

"He didn't stay for very long. He tied us up—I don't remember much about that, it all happened so fast—and then he climbed into the front seat. We drove for a few blocks, then the driver slipped some money into his hand and he got out. His name was like…Lee Wrangler? Or George Lee? I don't know exactly."

"Levi Washington?" Jordan suggested.

"Yeah, that's it. Where did I get George Lee from?"

"Because you were thinking of jeans and presidents," said Jordan. While Kaitlin laughed at that, he pulled out his notebook and wrote down Levi's name; that way he wouldn't forget to tell his captain to arrest and interrogate Levi at the first possible opportunity. Then the smile faded from Kaitlin's face and she resumed her story.

"Anyway, then we drove for a really long time. Finally we got to that office building or whatever and he forced us to get out and go down the stairs. He said he would kill us if we tried anything stupid. When he left to get Willow's cell phone to make her call her parents, I told her that I had gotten a glimpse of the street signs when he forced us out of the van and to try and work that into the conversation as a time."

"You are my daughter," Jordan said with a smile. "What happened after Willow hung up?"

"He tied us up to the boiler in the corner and said he had some business to take care of. Then he left. Willow and I tried everything we could, but neither of us could get loose."

Jordan did the math in his head; the business that Jonathan had been taking care of was helping them trace the call between Levi and Detective Taylor.

"Let me guess: he came back about thirty minutes later in a panic."

"How did you know that?" Kaitlin asked.

"I'll tell you later," Jordan said. "You're the one doing the talking right now."

"Right. Well yeah, he seemed really spooked. He paced around his room with that knife of his and kept muttering to himself about light and shadows. Willow and I thought he was going to kill us right then and there."

That was the first time that Kaitlin's voice broke and her fear showed through.

"You're doing great, sweetheart. Just a little bit more."

Kaitlin took a deep breath and continued.

"Finally he just decided to take Willow and go. He was about to cut her loose and then he stopped and got this evil smile on his face. He went through my bag until he found my cell phone and that's when he made me call you. He put it on speakerphone so that he could listen too. I guess he somehow knew that you were involved in this case and he wanted to taunt you. I almost wish you hadn't answered the phone. It would have been so much easier to lie over a voicemail."

"You did just fine. All those hours in drama paid off."

"Thanks," she said absently. "Anyway, after I hung up he made me stand on the other side of the room while he left with Willow. I told you the rest of it."

She looked very tired now.

"Come on," Jordan said. "You've been through a lot today and I just put you through even more. Let's check out those cots."

Kaitlin followed him willingly enough, and Jordan found a blanket for her. He stood up to leave, but Kaitlin caught hold of his wrist.

"Wait, Dad. I know you have work to do and everything and I understand why it's so important. But do you think you can stay here until I fall asleep?"

"Course I will," Jordan answered, pulling a straight-backed wooden chair over and settling himself in beside her bed. "I'm not going anywhere."

She smiled at him and was out within five minutes. All the worry disappeared from her face as she slept; the last time Jordan had watched that transformation, Kaitlin had been just a baby. He sat there just staring at her and then he heard someone whisper his name from the doorway. It was Longhorn, beckoning him outside.

Jordan got up quietly, careful not to disturb Kaitlin's rest, and went outside into the hallway.

"Any news?"

"Yes, but you won't like it."

"Willow?" Jordan asked, immediately assuming the worst.

"No, don't worry about that. She's alive. So is Jonathan. They found them both, but Jon's refusing to speak to anybody except you. He's got a knife to Willow's neck, says he'll kill her and then himself if you don't get there within thirty minutes."

Jordan turned around and took one last look at his daughter, sleeping peacefully now. "Guess I'd better get going then. Where are they?"

"Central Park. And what makes you think you're going alone? I'm driving. One of the rookies you just met will look after your daughter."

"Thanks, Charles. My wife's on her way, too."

Jordan wished he could be there to see his wife as well, but he knew that wasn't an option. He had work to do.

Chapter 22

IT WAS A twenty-minute drive to Central Park from the police station, but Longhorn got them there in fifteen. He explained the situation on the way.

"They went to Jon's house but he wasn't there. But one of the detectives found this huge map of Central Park, with pictures of the victims tacked up in a half-circle. Stonehenge, just like you said. When they got to the park, he had just finished setting everything up."

"What all did he have to set up exactly?" Jordan asked, fearing the answer.

"Life-sized photographs of all his victims, arranged so that the shadows fell just the right way. In the middle of all this, there's a big rock. That's where he's sitting with Willow, apparently."

"Hold on," Jordan murmured. "Kaitlin's not dead. He would need another victim to complete the circle."

"And he had one. She looked like she had just gone for a jog in the park. She must have been the first blond woman he saw."

"And Willow had to watch him do that?" Jordan was horrified at the very thought. What a thing for anybody to have to witness, let alone a young teenager.

"Yes. And now she's the one in danger of being killed."

"She's going to be his final victim," Jordan said. It was just as he'd feared. But he had made Willow's parents a promise, and he planned on keeping it. Besides, he didn't know if he could face telling his daughter that while she slept, he had let her best friend come to harm. She would have a hard time forgiving him and he would have an even harder time forgiving himself.

"No she won't," Longhorn said. "Because we're going to stop him before he can do anything."

They had arrived at the place where Jon Hall was. To Jordan's dismay, there was already a large crowd of passersby forming. They needed all their officers focused on the task at hand, not distracted by crowd control. And the last thing they needed was civilian casualties. Longhorn correctly interpreted the look on Jordan's face as he took in the scene, which was exactly as Longhorn had described to him.

"Leave the crowds to me," he said as they both got out of the car. "You do what you have to."

In response, Jordan grasped his shoulder briefly and flashed a smile of gratitude. Then he stepped slowly forward, letting his gun holster show, but also letting Jon see that his hands were far away from it. He stopped just outside the circle of life-sized cutouts, thinking that the scene was easily as creepy as any horror movie he had ever seen, if not more so. It was even worse when he remembered that one of the bodies was not a cutout at all. The grass was darkened around the latest victim, and yet nobody seemed to be looking at her. All of their attention was focused on the man with the knife. If fame and attention was what Jonathan wanted, he was certainly getting it.

"Hello, Jon. Hello, Willow."

Maybe it was Jordan's imagination, but it seemed like a sort of hush fell over the crowd of law enforcement officials and civilians surrounding them. Jon made no response to Jordan's greeting, but Willow looked up at him. She didn't say a word, but her eyes spoke loudly enough on their own. They were pleading, terrified. Jordan tried to communicate some kind of comfort through his own eyes, but he only looked at Willow for a second or two. Then he turned his attention back to Jon.

"I was told you wanted to speak with me?" Jordan continued, addressing only Jonathan, acting like the crowd around them didn't exist, acting like even Willow didn't exist.

"I need a witness before this thing happens. You," he barked suddenly at one of the young rookies who was standing behind Jordan at the hood of one of the police cars. "What time is it? And be specific."

The rookie looked to Reggie, who nodded very slightly. "8:01," he said.

"Eleven minutes, then. That's how much time we have together before Willow and I go."

"You won't be going anywhere, I'm afraid," said Jordan, keeping his voice perfectly calm. And before Jonathan could have time to process that threat, he spoke again. "What's this event that you keep talking about? What's happening in eleven minutes?"

"You've figured out everything else. Why should I tell you?"

"I haven't figured out everything," Jordan admitted. "Vast portions of it, yes. But I do still have questions. I know why you grabbed Willow—she's Irish, just like all your other victims have been. But Willow has real Irish blood in her veins; that's why you saved her for last. Why my daughter, though? No Irish in her."

"She was there," Jonathan said simply. "It was a matter of wrong place, wrong time. And she was the perfect height and weight to cast the right shadow. I actually planned to use her to complete the circle; but when I realized she was your daughter, I decided she would better serve as a distraction. You would desperately be searching for her while I was busy killing her little friend here."

"Well your plan didn't work," said Jordan. "You've already committed one murder tonight, but you won't be killing anyone else."

"Oh but I will, Detective. Look at you hiding back there in the shadows, scared to come and face me. You really think you can stop me doing what I came here to do? No, you're just here to serve your purpose as my witness. I don't know what's going to happen myself. That's what makes it exciting."

A genuine boyish grin spread across Jonathan's face, and it made Detective Jordan want to either shiver or vomit. He held himself back from doing either.

"You keep calling me a witness. But don't I at least deserve to know what I'm supposed to be witnessing?"

"I'm really disappointed in you, you know that?" said Jonathan. "What do you actually even know? Just tell me that much."

"I'll make you a deal, first," Jordan began, but Jonathan cut him off.

"No. No deals. You are not going to change my mind here. This is happening, there's nothing you can do to stop it, and you need to accept that and prepare yourself for what's coming."

As Jonathan spoke, he removed his blade from Willow's neck and waved it wildly through the air in agitation. He still kept his other hand tightly wound in Willow's hair, and she was smart enough to not try and escape. The knife was soon settled back into its position at her throat, but Jordan took note of the situation just the same. Maybe the best strategy would be to get Jonathan a little irritated. Not too much—then things could go south quickly—but just enough to keep him distracted, and not thinking about what he was doing with that knife. Now Jordan just wished there was some way of passing this little insight on to Longhorn without Jonathan noticing. But that, of course, was impossible. He would just have to trust in Longhorn's intellect, and that of the other officers grouped behind him.

"All right, Jonathan. We'll have it your way. No deals. But if I tell you what I know, you have to tell me the rest of it."

"Tick, tock. Start talking. What do you know?"

And Jordan thought that was the closest thing to an agreement he would get.

"I know that this has something to do with Stonehenge. The way you killed your victims, the way you made sure the knife cast just the right shadow. You're quite the photographer, clearly. And the last victim will be Willow—that was your plan at least, but that's not going to happen. But you saved her for last because you need the perfect sacrifice to be able to get to the next world."

"You know more than I thought," Jon said after a moment's pause.

"What I still don't get is the timing of it all," said Jordan. "My partner and I did a little research, and we know that the summer solstice is when the sun strikes the center of Stonehenge, the ancient Druidic altar where human sacrifices were made. You're just over a month too early."

"You're only half right. Yes, when the sun strikes the correct angle and all the shadows align, that's when the veil between worlds is thinnest and someone could cross over. Someone like me for instance. But the summer solstice is the important date in Europe. Here in New York we do things differently."

Jordan frowned, thinking hard. Something in what he was hearing sparked his memory a little, but he couldn't quite put his finger on it just yet. He knew he had to keep talking, but now only three quarters of his mind was actually focused on the conversation. The rest was desperately searching for the missing link.

"But why would you want to cross over to this other world? I mean I know this one isn't perfect—if it was, I would be out of a job—but how can you be sure that what's over there is any better?"

"Because I was told about it," Jon said, eyes lifting toward the sky. He watched the slowly sinking sun for a moment and the knife drifted away from Willow's throat again. Then he snapped his eyes back to the detective in front of him.

"Who told you?" Jordan asked. But he only asked because it was the logical next step in the conversation. His mind was buzzing. The time…why did he ask about the time? And why this particular location in Central Park?

"My grandfather. My full-blooded Irish grandfather. He was driving me back to my parents' house when I was eight years old, and we got in a car accident. We were hit head-on by some guy who was fleeing from the police. My grandfather died that night, with me watching him go. Just imagine that, being eight years old and watching somebody die, knowing there's nothing you can do."

Were those tears that Jordan saw forming in Jonathan's eyes, or was it merely a trick of the light? And suddenly, with a force that hit him almost like a physical blow, the pieces came together.

"So now you want to cross over to see him again. Using the power of Manhattanhenge to do it."

Jon looked impressed in spite of himself. Jordan was very glad he'd remembered the news story from a week before. About how the sun was going to align perfectly with the street grid of New York City, just like it aligned with the rocks of Stonehenge on the summer solstice.

"Smart man," said Jon.

"Did your grandfather tell you about the Druids as well? Did he pass on stories that his grandfather passed on to him?"

"And so on down the line, yes. But I knew the information couldn't be entirely trusted, being passed down like that. So I educated myself, first by spending hours in the library and then by sitting for hours at a time in front of a computer screen. I know this will work. And it must be nearly time now."

Now it was Jordan who asked what time it was, and Longhorn who answered him. It was 8:10.

"Two minutes. Years of effort and it will all be over in a matter of seconds." Jon sounded unbelieving. But not unsure of himself. No, he was perfectly confident. He stroked Willow's hair absentmindedly and raised his knife so it caught the light.

"It will be over for both of us," he whispered. Then his grip on Willow tightened and he bent her over the rock so that her blood would splash onto it, preparing the way for him to leave this world and enter the next.

The shadows crept forward as the sun sank to the very edge of the horizon.

Chapter 23

JORDAN'S PISTOL WAS in his hand, with the safety off and his finger on the trigger. He vaguely wondered how it had gotten there. Jon had his back turned to him and was admiring the way the light shown on his knife as he raised it to strike. Willow was screaming for all she was worth, people in the crowd yelling with her. But he forced himself to tune it all out and listen only to the sound of his own breathing and his own heartbeat. He knew he had only seconds to act.

He aimed carefully and squeezed off a single shot.

It hit directly on its target—Jonathan's right elbow, which was raised above his head holding the knife. He dropped it, and also let go of Willow's hair, reflexively cupping his left hand around the shattered joint of his right arm. He still tried to make a grab for the knife, but it was over. About ten police officers rushed forward and tackled him to the ground.

It was over. Jordan tried to let that sink in. He realized his gun was still raised, and lowered it slowly and put it back in his holster.

"Nice work, Mark," said a voice behind him. He turned and saw Braxton there. "That was a heck of a shot."

"I would have aimed a bit more at head level," said Longhorn. "Especially if he had kidnapped my daughter and her best friend."

"If I had killed him, he would have gotten what he wanted. This way he has to wait a little while. He deserves to live with what he's done."

Sirens blared behind them as two ambulances arrived, one for Jon and one for Willow.

"Do you want to be part of the escort group going to the hospital with that piece of scum?" asked Reggie Thyme, jogging up to them slightly out of breath. He had been one of the ones to tackle Jon to the ground.

"To be honest, no," said Jordan. "I have something else I need to do."

Reggie nodded his understanding and then walked away, snapping orders at his subordinates as he went. Jordan turned to Longhorn.

"Can I have a ride back to the police station? I'd like to see my daughter."

Back at Longhorn's precinct, Jordan looked in on his daughter, now deeply asleep and looking extremely peaceful. He marveled at the fact that she was safe; it was as if, even though he had played a part in her rescue, it still hadn't quite sunk in. But he did know one thing for sure: this was a night that he would well remember.

Made in the USA
Lexington, KY
24 October 2019

55801810R00081